"The ceremony starts in less than an hour!"

Richard held up a finger. "Correction, Annabelle. The ceremony was going to start in less than an hour."

"I suppose it would be too much to hope that we could get the body cleared out and still pull off the wedding?" I bit the edge of my lip. "It's not like there's any blood."

Richard put his hand on his hip. "Somehow I think that a dangling corpse will put a damper on the festivities, blood or not."

Praise for LAURA DURHAM's Annabelle Archer Mysteries

"A perfect marriage of murder and mirth ... [that] sparkles like a champagne cocktail."
Nora Charles

"Delightful mystery.... Cozy readers will love this invitation to a wedding to die for."
Nancy Martin, author of *Drop Dead Blonde*

"Laura Durham and her flair for witty characters and murder amidst matrimony are a match made in mystery heaven."
Ellen Byerrum, author of *Hostile Makeover*

"Laura Durham has given her readers [a] reason to celebrate.
Elaine Viets, author of *Just Murdered*

Annabelle Archer Mysteries
by Laura Durham

To Love and to Perish
For Better or Hearse
Better off Wed

LAURA DURHAM

To
LOVE
And To
PERISH

AN ANNABELLE ARCHER MYSTERY

AVON BOOKS
An Imprint of HarperCollinsPublishers

This is a work of fiction. Names, characters, places, and incidents are products of the author's imagination or are used fictitiously and are not to be construed as real. Any resemblance to actual events, locales, organizations, or persons, living or dead, is entirely coincidental.

AVON BOOKS
An Imprint of HarperCollins*Publishers*
10 East 53rd Street
New York, New York 10022-5299

First Avon Books paperback printing: February 2007

Avon Trademark Reg. U.S. Pat. Off. and in Other Countries, Marca Registrada, Hecho en U.S.A.
HarperCollins® is a registered trademark of HarperCollins Publishers.

Printed in the U.S.A.

10 9 8 7 6 5 4 3 2 1

For my brother, James,
whose quick wit is matched only by his great kindness

Acknowledgments

Huge thanks to all the readers who have been so supportive and encouraging. Special thanks to Alison, Anne, and Monte for the great stories; to Ric for the constant inspiration; to Jenny for helping me get it right; to Jessica and the women at Promise for the great party; to the Rector Lane Irregulars for the good advice; to Susan for making traveling fun; to The Mystery Chicks for being such a great bunch to hang out with in cyberspace; and to my dear friend, Noreen, for believing in me.

Thanks to my wonderful agent, Peter Rubie, and to the fabulous folks at Avon—Jeremy, Danielle, and my amazing editor, Sarah Durand. As always, thanks to my wonderfully supportive husband and family. I couldn't do it without you.

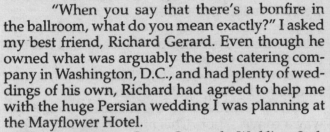

Chapter 1

"When you say that there's a bonfire in the ballroom, what do you mean exactly?" I asked my best friend, Richard Gerard. Even though he owned what was arguably the best catering company in Washington, D.C., and had plenty of weddings of his own, Richard had agreed to help me with the huge Persian wedding I was planning at the Mayflower Hotel.

The prestigious *Grace Ormonde Wedding Style* magazine was covering the event for its spring issue, and thanks to Richard the word had spread around town faster than it took for his spray-on tan to set. He said that if I could pull off a wedding this elaborate, it would put my company, Wedding Belles, on the Who's Who list of wedding planners for good. Naturally he would be the caterer of choice for all my weddings once I hit the big time.

"You know very well that I'm not given to dramatics, Annabelle." Richard fanned himself with a lime green and hot pink striped silk handkerchief. "I meant exactly what I said. The father of the groom is building himself a bonfire in the middle of the room."

I motioned for Richard to lower his voice. We stood near the bank of brass elevators in the brightly decorated hotel lobby. A lighted green garland was draped from the balconies that overlooked the gilded lobby, and a Christmas tree decorated entirely with wide swaths of deep red silk and burgundy organza stood across from us, next to the wooden concierge desk. The hotel seemed even busier than usual with holiday visitors, and people were beginning to stare at us. I hoped they weren't wedding guests.

"Just when I thought this day couldn't get much worse," I grumbled. "I already had a run-in with Carolyn Crabbe."

Richard's eyes widened. "The Grand Dame of wedding planning spoke to you?"

"If you consider warning me to stay out of her way a conversation. This must be Wedding Planner Central today because I also bumped into Gail Gordan and Byron Wolfe."

Richard glanced around him and winced. "I hate it when there are multiple weddings at the same site. That means multiple brides and wedding planners."

"Hello?" I said. "I'm a wedding planner, remember?"

"I don't mean you, darling. You're perfection. But Gail and Byron are too puffed up for my taste. You'd think they were the only planners in town doing high-end parties."

"Well, they were both perfectly nice to me. Maybe a bit stressed, but their bride was running late to the church so I understood completely. Carolyn was out and out mean."

"Did she threaten you with her pointer?"

"She really uses a pointer? I thought that was just a story people had made up to make her seem scarier."

Richard leaned in. "The last I heard, she was still using one of those expandable metal pointers to direct vendors at weddings."

I gulped. "No, she didn't threaten me with her pointer. Yet."

"I wouldn't worry about her. She's just jealous that your wedding is getting media attention and her wedding is in the smallest ballroom in the hotel." Richard gave a dismissive wave with his hands. "All the big wigs in the industry earned their chops being tormented by her. Trust me, darling. Being threatened by Carolyn Crabbe is a step in the right direction."

"That's one way to look at it." I rubbed my temples. "I'm still going to steer clear of her. Now how far along has our father of the groom gotten with his bonfire?"

Richard placed a hand on his hip. "I don't know. He's got wood in a pile. Do I look like I was a Boy Scout to you?"

"Not exactly," I admitted.

"I mean, really." He gave a quiet snicker. "Can you imagine me in a green polyester uniform?"

"I think the Girl Scouts wear green, not the Boy Scouts."

"Then do I look like I was a Girl Scout?" Richard held up a hand before I could speak. "Don't even think of answering that. All I know is that the man is hell-bent on starting a fire."

"I guess he isn't in favor of the marriage." I tucked a few loose strands of long auburn hair back into my wilted French twist. We'd been running around the hotel for the past six hours getting ready for the wedding, and I knew I looked as frazzled as I felt. I was glad that I'd worn one of my comfortable and practical black pantsuits with a shimmery silk top the color of cranberries. I didn't think I could bear wearing a dress and heels for this long.

Richard ran a hand through his dark, choppy hair. "Apparently he's paying tribute to his ancient Zoroastrian heritage. A sacred flame is one of their wedding traditions."

"Whatever happened to traditions like throwing rice?" I muttered, wondering why I couldn't have one wedding where someone didn't forget the marriage license, leave the wedding dress in a taxi, or set the ballroom on fire.

"They're throwing rice?" My assistant, Kate, stepped out of the elevator in front of us with her ten page wedding schedule in hand. Kate's blond bob had lost its usual bounce and her pink lipstick had worn off. Although she also wore black, her short black cocktail dress and cropped jacket could never be considered conservative. No matter how many hours we were on our feet, Kate dressed to show off her legs and her absurdly expensive high heels. I could bet money that she was the only wedding planner in town who worked in

Jimmy Choos. "When did that get added to the schedule?"

"I'd like to see people throw rice again." Richard tapped his chin. "Kitsch is in, you know."

I rolled my eyes. "There's no rice."

Kate shoved her schedule in the pocket of her black jacket. "Good. If I have to make any more marks on my timeline, I won't be able to see the paper."

"We do have a bit of a problem, though." I pulled Kate closer to me and dropped my voice to a whisper. "The father of the bride is building a sacred fire in the ballroom. Can you go back up to the bride's suite and keep her there until I call you? I don't want her to see her ceremony go up in smoke."

Kate cringed. "That's what I came to tell you. Fern is bringing the bride down for pictures."

At least the bride was in good hands. Fern was the city's wedding hair guru and took pride in fussing over his brides up until the last possible second. The elevator doors opened and Fern rushed out. He'd pulled his dark hair back in a severe ponytail, and clouds of white tulle spilled over his arms.

"The bride took the next elevator," he explained, dragging the cathedral-length veil behind him. "No one else could fit in there with that huge dress. I was afraid munchkins were going to start running out from beneath her skirt."

"Can you keep her away from the ballroom?" I asked. "Kate and I need to take care of a little issue before she sees the room."

"An issue? Say no more." Fern handed his arm-load of tulle to Richard. "Hold this for a second, will you, doll?"

Richard spluttered a few words of protest before his mouth gaped open. "What are you wearing?"

"Do you like the jacket?" Fern turned to let us admire the long fitted merlot-colored jacket with embroidered lapels. "It seemed appropriate for a holiday wedding."

Fern lived to coordinate with his brides' weddings. I feared that one day he would show up in a matching bridesmaid's gown.

"Not the jacket." Richard pushed a layer of tulle off his face. "Is that a skirt?"

Fern smoothed what appeared to be a black pair of pants with a wraparound front. "It's called a man skirt and I'll have you know that it's Gaultier."

Richard raised an eyebrow. "I don't remember seeing this in the collection. Is it last season?"

Fern gave him a scandalized look. "Bite your tongue. This was the talk of the fall collection."

"Don't we have a fire to put out?" Kate tugged on my sleeve. "Literally."

I turned to Fern. "Can you keep the bride far away from the ballroom for ten minutes while we stop her father from burning the building down with his ceremonial bonfire?"

"You can count on me, honey." Fern winked. "I'm a master at creating distractions."

"That's putting it mildly." Richard passed the billowing tulle back to Fern, and then motioned for me and Kate to follow him with a jerk of his head. "Let's go extinguish a sacred flame."

Kate and I followed Richard down the long

black and white marble hallway that cut through the middle of the hotel. We went down a few steps and passed the open air restaurant, Café Promenade, which had an enormous crystal chandelier hanging in the center and sleek arrangements of white and red amaryllis on the tables. We continued down the hallway, passing tall fir trees decorated with white lights and red ribbon every few feet.

Richard stopped in front of a set of tall white doors that had garland draped across the top and tied at the corners with red sashes. A brass plaque to the side of the door read: GRAND BALLROOM.

"I don't hear fire alarms," Kate said. "That's a good sign."

Richard opened the doors, and we were met with total darkness.

"Why are the lights off?" I asked, stepping inside the room and groping along the wall for the lighting control panel.

"Do you think the lighting company blew a fuse when they were setting up?" Kate started looking for a switch on the other side of the door.

I groaned. The bride's favorite part of the wedding decor was the specially designed monogram that we planned to project in light on the dance floor. "The wedding gods must be punishing me."

"Be careful," Richard said. "Don't forget the steps."

"Here they are," Kate said. "You could kill yourself on these in the dark."

Richard screamed and we heard him tumble to the floor. "Don't forget the second set of steps, either."

"Are you okay?" I asked, holding my arms out in front of me to find a railing.

"I hate hotels," Richard complained.

"The lights aren't on the main wall. They're behind a curtain somewhere," Kate said, her voice getting farther away. "Found them!"

The ballroom lights flooded the room. I blinked a few times as my eyes adjusted to the sudden brightness. The holiday theme of garland continued in the ballroom, with swags of lighted greenery on each of the wood and iron balconies that jutted out over the room. We'd hung red and gold Christmas balls from clear wire throughout the room at different levels, and they sparkled in the light from the dangling chandeliers. I strained to see across the room to the stage where the ceremony would take place, but my eyes were drawn above the platform to a long piece of fabric hanging from the center balcony.

"I thought we weren't allowed to hang anything from the balcony railings," Kate said as she walked over, and then paled a few shades. "Is that what I think it is?"

I nodded as I watched Carolyn Crabbe's limp body slowly twist from the end of a long white veil.

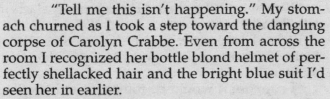

Chapter 2

"Tell me this isn't happening." My stomach churned as I took a step toward the dangling corpse of Carolyn Crabbe. Even from across the room I recognized her bottle blond helmet of perfectly shellacked hair and the bright blue suit I'd seen her in earlier.

Richard opened his mouth and then closed it again. I had rarely seen him speechless.

"Is that really ...?" Kate's voice faded and she clasped her hand over her mouth.

I looked away, grateful that the body wasn't facing us. "It's Carolyn Crabbe all right."

"We should get her down from there." Kate's voice was barely a whisper. "How awful to be hanging like that."

"I think she's beyond saving, Kate," Richard said. "But why don't you go get Security? Annabelle and I will wait with the body."

Kate looked at Carolyn and gave one last shudder before hurrying out of the ballroom and closing the door behind her.

I took a long, deep breath to keep from being sick and looked away from the body and around the ballroom. Rows of gold chairs were covered in sheer burgundy organza and draped with strands of iridescent beads. We'd covered the stage in heavy gold damask and tall arrangements of crimson flowers perched at the corners. The slightly raised ceremonial platform, or *sofreh*, for the Persian ceremony was filled from end to end with ornate gold candelabra, bowls of honey, trays of sweets, and a large gilded copy of the Koran on a pedestal.

"Now what?" I sighed. "The ceremony starts in less than an hour."

Richard held up a finger. "Correction, Annabelle. The ceremony *was* going to start in less than an hour."

"I suppose it would be too much to hope that we could get the body cleared out and still pull off the wedding?" I bit the edge of my lip. "It's not like there's any blood."

Richard put a hand on his hip. "Somehow I think that a dangling corpse will put a damper on the festivities, blood or not."

"Maybe we could keep Carolyn's death quiet and move the ceremony to another room," I said, making a mental calculation of how long it would take to move the numerous items on the ceremonial platform, and felt a huge headache coming on.

"Does the platform for the ceremony have wheels that I don't know about?" Richard narrowed his eyes at me. "We could always roll it out the door and into another room."

"Believe me, if I could fit it through the doors, I would."

Richard shook his head at me. "I was only joking, Annabelle. I doubt the hotel would look too favorably at having a ceremony wheeled through their lobby."

"Nothing else can fit in that lobby." Fern's voice startled me as he walked into the ballroom behind us. "There are bridesmaids as far as the eye can see. For once I think the Don Juan of the wedding photography world has his hands full. I don't think even Maxwell can flirt with that many girls at one time."

I whirled around. So much for keeping this disaster low profile. "What are you doing here? I thought you were with the bride."

"She's about to leave for her monument portraits so I thought I'd come take a peek at the room before ..." Fern did a double take when he caught sight of Carolyn Crabbe dangling in midair, then a look of comprehension crossed his face. "So this is why you wanted to keep people out of the room. Very clever, you two. The story about the bonfire was a nice touch."

Richard sucked in his breath. "You think we had something to do with this?"

"Well, that is Carolyn Crabbe, right?" Fern tapped his chin and looked pointedly at Richard. "And she did tell people that you were difficult to work with a few years back, didn't she?"

A flush crawled up Richard's face and a vein in his temple began to pulse. "What? I never heard that."

"Oh?" Fern gave a nervous giggle. "I could have sworn that you had. Never mind. It clearly isn't important now."

"We found her like this," I explained. "We had nothing to do with her death. It looks like she hung herself anyway."

"Talk about letting your clients push you over the edge." Fern nudged me with his elbow.

"You think this is a suicide?" Richard asked me. "Are you deranged?"

"What? You don't?" I looked from him to Fern and back again.

"Don't you find it a bit odd that Carolyn would hang herself while she's running a wedding?" Richard glanced at the deceased and lowered his voice. "She may have been an unpleasant, over-bearing, controlling diva, but she never let anything ruin a wedding."

Fern bobbed his head in agreement. "She could be an unbearable prima donna, but she was always a professional about it."

Ringing endorsements if I'd ever heard them.

"So you two think someone got her up on the balcony, tied a veil around her neck, and pushed her off?"

"It would be easy enough to slip the noose around her neck while her back was turned and push her over the edge," Fern said. "And, trust me, tulle is stronger than it looks."

Richard cocked an eyebrow at Fern. "You know this hypothetically, of course."

Fern crossed his arms in front of his chest. "Of course."

"So it had to be someone who knew her," I said.

"Everyone knew Carolyn," Richard reminded me. "She's been in this business for almost twenty years. There's no one she didn't know."

"Or didn't tick off," Fern added.

I sighed. "I'm glad I'm not the only one."

"She couldn't stand other wedding planners." Fern nodded solemnly. "When did you have a run-in with the darling diva?"

I gave a dismissive wave. "It was nothing. Carolyn wasn't too happy that we were going to be using the hallway for portraits. She wanted to set up her escort card table early, and our photos were ruining her plans. She warned me not to get in her way."

"You mean today?" Fern's voice barely rose above a whisper. "You had it out with Carolyn right before she died?"

Richard rubbed his temples. "Maybe we shouldn't mention this to anyone else."

"Why not?" I said. "I didn't have anything to do with this. I barely even knew the woman. Anyway, she's the one who threatened me."

"You know how touchy the police get about people turning up murdered after an argument." Richard shrugged. "They might jump to the wrong conclusion."

"He's right." Fern patted my arm. "You don't want anyone saying you killed the competition, Annabelle."

The ballroom doors flew open and a loud voice filled the room. "I knew I'd find you here, Annabelle Archer. You didn't think you'd get away with this, did you?"

Chapter 3

"Giancarlo?" I strained to make out the figure in the doorway.

"I've been looking for you everywhere." The stocky banquet captain strode into the room. "A bonfire is against the fire code, even if it is a sacred part of the ceremony."

"What?" I'd almost forgotten about what had seemed like a huge crisis only moments ago.

"Didn't you tell her?" Giancarlo's dark eyebrows were furrowed into a single line as he turned to Richard, and then his mouth dropped open.

"We have a bigger problem than a fire code violation," I explained.

The imperious banquet captain staggered back a few steps. "My God! Is that Carolyn Crabbe? What is she doing in here? Her wedding is in the East Room."

"I don't think being in the wrong ballroom is Carolyn's biggest concern right now," Richard muttered.

"We have to get her down from there." Giancarlo waved his arms over his head. "It's very bad for the hotel to have a body hanging from the balcony of our ballroom."

"I'd say it's worse for Carolyn," Fern whispered to me behind his hand.

"You shouldn't move the body." Richard hurried after Giancarlo as he headed for the stairs to the second level. "The police will be here any minute and they won't want the crime scene tampered with. Trust me on this one."

"The police?" Giancarlo shook his head vehemently. "Oh, no. We can't have the police in here. They will make a huge scene. We have too many holiday tourists in the hotel for that."

"Well, you have had a death in the hotel," Richard insisted, matching Giancarlo step for step. "You have to let the police do their job."

The argument continued in muffled voices as they disappeared into the stairwell at the end of the room.

"This I have to see." Fern clapped his hands together. "The city's toughest banquet captain going head-to-head with Richard."

"It does seem like a fair fight," I agreed.

Fern rubbed his hands together gleefully. "If only we had popcorn."

Richard and Giancarlo appeared above us on the balcony with Carolyn hanging below them.

Giancarlo leaned over and grabbed the tulle. "I'm going to pull her up."

"You can't disturb the body," Richard said, trying to push him out of the way. "It's against the law."

"No one tells me what to do in my hotel!" Giancarlo bellowed, his face purple from exertion.

I tugged Fern's sleeve. "Maybe we should go get help."

"Are you kidding?" He didn't tear his eyes off the grappling men. "And miss this? Next they're going to be pulling each other's hair."

I put a hand over my eyes. "I hope the police get here before we have two crimes to report."

"They're on their way," Kate said as she walked back into the ballroom. "What's all the racket?"

I motioned to Giancarlo trying to pull Carolyn's body up with one arm while holding Richard in a headlock with the other.

"Let go!" Richard screamed. "If you rip my Prada jacket, I'll sue."

Kate's eyes widened. "I don't think I've ever seen Richard fight. Talk about a fish running out of water."

"You mean a fish out of water?" I asked. Kate loved using colorful expressions, but I had yet to hear her get one quite right.

"That, too." Kate didn't take her eyes off the fight. "Oh, I bumped into Margery and Lucille in the hallway. They're looking for Carolyn."

Margery and Lucille had been Carolyn's assistants for almost as long as she'd been planning weddings. Although they were the same age as Carolyn, neither woman had ever seemed to mind playing second fiddle to the domineering diva. I'd always found the assistants much more personable than the grande dame herself.

"What did you tell them?" I asked.

Kate darted a glance behind her. "Nothing,

but I think they were a bit suspicious of me."

"Yoo hoo!" a warbling voice called out from the door. Carolyn's assistant, Lucille, stood in the doorway in a navy blue knit suit with gold buttons. She wore her white hair cut short and immaculately arranged. Lucille struck me as the grandmotherly type of wedding planner who excelled at holding hands and wiping away tears. The perfect balance for Carolyn's abrasive personality.

"Lucille." I ran to intercept her before she could see Carolyn. "How nice to see you."

Kate joined me in pushing her back toward the hall. "Let's step outside to chat."

"If you don't let go of me this instant, I'm going to call my lawyer!" Richard shrieked from the balcony.

"I'd like to see you try it!" Giancarlo screamed back, and hoisted the veil up a few inches. Carolyn's body lurched up and spun around to face us.

"Carolyn!" Lucille cried out and pushed past us toward the swaying corpse.

"Crap." I ran after Lucille.

"Did you find her?" Margery, Carolyn's other assistant, poked her head in the door.

"I've almost got her," Giancarlo huffed as he leaned back and pulled hard, swiping at Richard with one fist.

"Lucille, get back here," Margery cried as Lucille ran around under Carolyn's swinging body.

"I can catch her." Lucille ran up onto the ceremony table with her arms stretched out. I covered my eyes as she trampled the ceremony arrangements.

"Put her back down or else." Richard dodged the enraged captain's blows as he tried to land a few kicks of his own.

Giancarlo stumbled forward and the veil slipped out of his hands. The body dropped a few feet and snapped back as all the slack gave way, and then the fabric of the veil began to rip. Giancarlo and Richard stopped grappling long enough to watch from above as Carolyn plummeted to the ground.

Lucille held her arms open as Carolyn fell on top of her, and she staggered for a second under the weight of the body before her knees buckled and she landed with a crunch on top of the elaborate ceremony platform. I watched through my fingers as Carolyn's head flopped face first in the bowl of honey.

Fern gasped and turned to me. "I must say, Annabelle. No one does weddings like you do."

Chapter 4

"I think it's safe to say that we won't be getting back in there any time soon," Kate said as the hotel security officers slammed the ballroom doors on us.

"Not that the ceremony is salvageable." I shook my head. "Almost everything got broken."

"Well, a dead body did land on top of the *sofreh*." Kate gave Richard a pointed look.

"Don't look at me," Richard said. "I told that despotic banquet captain not to fiddle with the body."

"What are we going to do without Carolyn?" Lucille sobbed into Margery's shoulder. "We have a wedding starting in ten minutes."

"Here, honey." Fern held out a hemstitched linen handkerchief with a flowery embroidered *F*, and then began to sniffle as he watched Lucille cry. He started to dab his own eyes with the handkerchief before Lucille could take it. "Here come the waterworks. I can't watch someone cry without crying myself."

Richard rolled his eyes. "Oh, for heaven's sake."

"At least you still have a wedding," I reassured the two older women. "Ours will have to be postponed for several hours, if it can even take place at all."

"It's not like you haven't done lots of weddings before." Kate patted Lucille on the back. "I know Carolyn is a huge loss, but you two will be fine."

"You never worked with Carolyn, did you?" Margery ran her fingers through her dark burgundy hair and looked at the floor. While Lucille stood out with her perfectly styled white hair and grandmotherly persona, Margery always looked a bit out of her element to me. With a nondescript brown suit, a dye job that made her hair look almost purple, and almost no makeup, she certainly didn't look like a high-profile wedding planner's assistant. I'd once heard Carolyn say that no bride would ever feel threatened by Margery. I wished I could say the same about Kate.

Lucille raised her head and wiped away her tears with the back of her hand. "She was such a perfectionist that she insisted on doing all the ceremonies herself. She liked to send the brides down the aisle personally, so Margery and I took care of details like putting out menu cards or loading people into buses."

"Sometimes she would let us help getting the ushers set up, but the processional was all hers," Margery added.

My eyes widened. Carolyn's assistants were at least thirty years older than me and they'd been working in weddings for the past twenty.

"You've never sent a bride down the aisle?"

"I wish you were that much of a control freak," Kate said so only I could hear. "I hate coordinating ceremony processionals."

I agreed. One part of wedding planning that I would never miss was the last nerve-wracking minutes before the bride walked down the aisle. It seemed like the majority of guests arrived in the final five minutes and had to be hurried to their seats in record time before lining up the mothers, grandmothers, and even stepmothers to be seated. Then the groomsmen were off down the aisle, followed by a gaggle of bridesmaids, the ring bearer and flower girl, who usually either began to cry or wet their pants. Then, finally, there was the bride. It told me a lot about Carolyn that she had insisted on running the processional herself for the past twenty years. She was clearly off her rocker.

"It's not hard to run a processional," I lied. "You'll be fine."

Richard rubbed his neck where Giancarlo had held him in a headlock. "It's not rocket science, that's for sure."

I shot him a look. "Thanks, Richard." I turned back to Lucille and Margery. "Do you have a list of who walks when?"

Margery produced a packet of folded pages from a leather portfolio.

"There you go," Richard said, waving a hand at the wedding timeline. "I've always said that as long as you have a good timeline, a trained monkey could run things. Right, Kate?"

"Absolutely ..." Kate began, then closed her

mouth and glared at Richard. "Very funny."

Richard stepped out of Kate's reach and scooted behind me. Before Kate could chase after him, a willowy blonde in a long forest-green bridesmaid's dress rushed across the hall from the East Room. Her eyes darted back and forth between Lucille and Margery.

"Aren't you with the wedding planner?" she asked, putting her hands on her hips. "Angela wants to know if we're going to start on time."

Lucille gave her a blank look. "Angela?"

The bridesmaid gave an impatient sigh and began tapping her foot. "The bride."

"Of course," Margery pushed Lucille off her shoulder and regained her composure. "We're on our way to start the ceremony."

"You'd better hurry." The girl tossed her long hair off her shoulder. "Because the ushers don't know what they're doing and everyone is standing around at the back. The carolers aren't even singing."

"Carolers?" Richard gave me a look that told me exactly what he thought of carolers singing at a wedding.

Lucille bobbed her head of perfectly coiffed white hair up and down. "The bride wanted a Dickensian feel to the wedding. A nice holiday touch, don't you think?"

"Nothing like a little Charles Dickens squalor and misery to put you in the wedding mood," Richard said under his breath.

"We're on our way," Margery called to the bridesmaid's back as she flounced off. She turned to me. "You have to help us."

"What?" I took a step back and shook my head.

"No. We have our own mess to deal with."

"It won't take very long," Margery begged, clutching my hands.

"Please," Lucille pleaded through red, puffy eyes. "We can't do this alone. Not after losing Carolyn in such a horrible way..." She collapsed into tears again.

"Of course we'll help you," Fern cried, and flung his arms around Margery and Lucille. He wiped his own tears away with a dramatic sweep of his handkerchief. "You can count on us, right, girls?"

I felt overwhelmed with the desire to beat Fern to death with his hairbrush.

Kate shrugged. "We might as well throw in the trowel and do it."

"Throw in the trowel?" Richard tapped his chin and smirked at me.

"Fine," I said. "But let's hurry. We still have to break the bad news to our bride before she hears it through the grapevine."

Lucille and Margery led the way to the East Room across the hall. The bridesmaid had been right. The wedding was total chaos. The room had been set up for the ceremony with rows of gold chairs with green velvet cushions, but no one sat in them. Guests mingled in the aisle while the groomsmen stood talking to each other against the wall of gold curtains in the back. A string quartet sat silently at the front of the room near the enormous gold mirror that took up most of the wall, while a group of costumed carolers huddled inside the door.

"Margery, you have the order that the groomsmen process in, right? Can you take care of them?"

Lucille shook her head at me and whispered, "She's blind as a bat without her glasses. She probably can't even tell the groomsmen apart."

I quickly formulated Plan B and turned to Kate. "You're the expert with men. Can you whip these groomsmen into shape and have them start seating guests?"

Kate eyed the group of tall tuxedo-clad men clustered in a corner and tugged the neckline of her top down. "Is the Pope Baptist?"

I was about to correct her but decided we didn't have time. She headed off in the direction of the groomsmen with her hips swaying from side to side.

I turned to Fern. "Can you handle the bridesmaids?"

"Are those tramps chewing gum?" Fern sucked in his breath. "Don't you worry, Annabelle. I'm going to take them to the hall and get them shaped up."

I smiled thinking about what Miss Bossy Boots Bridesmaid was in for.

I turned back to Margery. "Why don't you tell the carolers to start singing and cue the processional music for the string quartet?"

"Should I go get the bride and the flower girls?" Lucille whispered to me once Margery had made a beeline for the carolers.

"That would be great, Lucille."

"Well, it looks like you've got this under control," Richard began, backing out of the room.

"Not so fast." I grabbed him by the sleeve. "I need you to help me with the bride and flower girls. I can't trust Lucille not to fall to pieces again."

"Fine," Richard said with a huff. "But I hope you know how much you owe me for today."

"I know, I know."

"This is giving the Martin wedding a run for its money."

"For the hundredth time, Richard, I had nothing to do with the cat theme."

"May I remind you that the invitation was issued by the couple's cats? That may have been the only time in the history of the world that the words 'Muffles' and 'Snuffy' have been engraved on Crane's paper."

Richard held the door for me as we went out into the hallway to meet the bride. "What on earth?" I stopped short, and he nearly crashed into me.

About a dozen little girls in white flower girl dresses with green velvet sashes were gathered in the hallway around the bride. Some wore floral halos and others carried round pomanders of crimson roses on ribbon strings. The angelic-looking flower girls were currently using the pomanders to whack each other, and at least half of the girls were crying. Lucille had a vacant smile on her face as she stood behind the bride, holding the cathedral length train. The petite bride had dark hair and pale white skin and looked equally dazed and unaffected by the wailing children. I wanted some of whatever she and Lucille were on.

I snaked my way through the children to Lucille. "How many flower girls are there exactly?"

"Ten, I think." Lucille glanced at the girls. "At

least there were ten. We might have lost one on the way here."

"Lost one?" My voice came out as barely a squeak.

"Annabelle." Richard pushed his way around the flower girls like they were lepers. "You know how I feel about children."

Richard wasn't fond of children or animals. Both were too unpredictable and messy for his liking.

"I know, but you can't leave me with them. Look how many there are."

"Exactly my point. This is like herding kittens."

Margery poked her head out of the ballroom door. "We're seating the mothers, and then sending the groomsmen down. The bridesmaids are next."

"Chests out, ladies." Fern clapped his hands as he led his now orderly line of bridesmaids to the door. "If you're going to wear a strapless gown, you might as well flaunt it a little. I saw a lot of single men in there. Work it, you two-bit hussies."

Not exactly the pep talk I gave bridesmaids, but Fern could get away with things that would get me fired on the spot.

"Help me line up the flower girls in pairs," I said to Richard as I pulled two girls by the hands and planted them behind the last bridesmaid. Richard guided two tiny girls into place with a fingertip on each of their backs.

"They won't bite you," I said.

He eyed the flower girls with suspicion. "You don't know that for sure."

We corralled the remaining girls into a semblance of a double line as the ballroom doors opened and

Fern started sending the bridesmaids down the aisle. One of the smallest flower girls began to cry and threw her arms around Richard's leg.

"Get it off! Get it off!" Richard shook his leg.

"Richard, calm down." I bent down to the little girl's level. "Don't you want to let go of the nice man and walk down the aisle?"

She shook her head and tightened her grasp on Richard. I looked up at Richard and shrugged my shoulders.

"What?" Richard returned my shrug. "I'm supposed to walk around like this for the rest of my life?"

"Can you help me with her veil, Annabelle?" Lucille called from behind the bride.

Richard grabbed my arm. "If you think you're going to leave me alone with this child, you're out of your mind, Annabelle."

"You can handle it, Richard. She can't be more than three years old. Anyway, I'll only be a few feet away from you."

Richard looked down at the little girl wiping her running nose on his pants, and he tightened his grip on me. "I'm warning you, Annabelle. If you take one more step, I will hunt you down to the ends of the earth."

Knowing Richard, even a witness relocation program wouldn't do me any good if I abandoned him with a wailing child clinging to his now sticky Prada pants.

I felt a hand on my shoulder and saw the color drain from Richard's face as a deep voice spoke from behind me. "I think you'd both better come with me."

Chapter 5

I turned to find Detective Mike Reese, a dark-haired cop who had a knack for turning up when things weren't going so great for me. I could never be sure whether the fear of being arrested or his good looks made my heart race. "Why am I not surprised you're here?"

He managed a weak grin. "I was going to say the exactly same thing. We need to talk about the death of Carolyn Crabbe."

"I swear I wasn't anywhere near the victim—" I began my protest.

Reese held up his hands. "Whoa. I know you weren't near the murder scene. We've already had several witnesses place you in the lobby before you found the body."

Richard pushed me out of the way and held his arms straight out in front of him. "Arrest me. Lock me up. Let the justice system have its way with me. Just get this creature off my leg."

Reese dropped his eyes to the tiny blond flower

girl who now sat sucking her thumb on Richard's shoe with one arm wrapped around his leg. The edges of his mouth quivered as he obviously strained to keep his composure. "We might need the jaws of life," he said, his eyes flashing with merriment.

Richard didn't smile, and I knew that I would be risking bodily harm if I laughed.

"We need to entice her with something," I said, glancing around me. Where had I left my emergency kit? I saw Fern shoo the last flower girl through the doors, and I mouthed a silent *Thank you* to him as I rushed around to help Lucille with the bride. I heard a loud fanfare as the bride started her walk down the aisle, Lucille following her into the ballroom, fluffing her train the whole way.

Richard pulled his wallet out of his inside jacket pocket and produced a stack of bills. "How about a twenty?"

Reese raised an eyebrow at him. "I don't think so."

"Well, I'm not giving her a fifty. That's extortion."

"I didn't mean to entice her with cash," I said. "She's a child, for crying out loud. We need to find some candy or something."

Richard replaced his wallet with a sniff. "Would have worked when I was a child."

"You were a child?" Fern asked as he joined us and gave Richard the once-over. "Hard to imagine."

Richard folded his arms in front of him. "I'm going to pretend I didn't hear that."

"How about a stick of gum?" Reese produced a slightly weathered piece from the pocket of his black wool blazer.

"It's worth a shot." I took the gum and bent down to the flower girl's level. "If you let go of the nice man, you can have this piece of gum."

She seemed to weigh her options for a moment, then nodded and simultaneously let go of Richard's leg and snatched the gum out of my fingers.

"Thank God," Richard sighed as the girl toddled off down the aisle after the bride.

"And she even made it down the aisle." I pointed as the errant flower girl reached the end of the aisle behind the bride, took a seat on the bride's train, and proceeded to unwrap her gum. The audience began to laugh. "Sort of."

Fern put an arm around my shoulders. "With ten flower girls, anything short of a citywide riot is a victory."

Kate slipped out of the ballroom and pulled the door closed behind her. "Not bad if I do say so myself." She caught sight of Reese and rolled her shoulders back. "Well, hello again."

Reese made a point to avert his eyes from her cleavage. An admirable feat considering Kate's dramatically low-cut dress.

"I'm glad you're all here," he said. "I need to ask you a few questions about Carolyn Crabbe."

"This won't take too long, will it?" I glanced nervously around the lobby. "Our bride still doesn't know that her wedding won't be happening and she's around here somewhere taking pictures."

"Don't worry." Kate pointed to her wedding

schedule. "She left to do photos at the monuments with Maxwell, remember? She won't be back for another thirty minutes at least."

I let out a long breath. It had slipped my mind in all the frenzy that the bride wanted photos with her bridesmaids in front of the Jefferson Memorial. Usually the Jefferson was a hot spot for photos in the spring when the cherry blossoms were in season, but this bride had insisted on photos there even though the trees were bare and it was close to freezing. More proof that brides could not be thwarted by logic or sanity.

"Let's go in the ballroom." Reese motioned for us to follow him across the hall, where the police had already put up swags of yellow crime scene tape. "I need for you to explain how things were before the crime scene was tampered with."

I swallowed hard as we entered the ballroom again and averted my eyes from the stage where officers now gathered around Carolyn's body. "She hung above the stage."

Reese nodded. "We figured that from where she landed."

"I told that banquet captain not to mess with the body, Detective," Richard said. "But he refused to listen to me."

Reese shook his head and frowned. "We have some officers questioning him right now. When we arrived we found him trying to drag the body off the stage. He may be facing some charges."

Kate shuddered. "He touched the corpse? Isn't it hard to move bodies once they've gone into rigor mortis?"

I looked at Kate in amazement and wondered

if she'd been watching *CSI* marathons again.

Reese looked impressed, too. "It might be hard to move the body if she'd been dead for very long, but the time of death was probably only minutes before you saw her."

I felt a chill go through my body. "You mean she'd just died when we walked in?"

Reese gave a curt nod of his head. "She was barely blue when we got here."

"Pretty," Richard muttered.

Reese rested his gaze on me. "Can you tell me anything else about what the victim looked like when you saw her?"

"It looked like she'd been hung by a bride's veil or at least the fabric used to make them," I said. "I didn't get a good look at her because she faced the other way most of the time."

"Until Richard and Giancarlo started fighting over the body and then she started spinning," Kate added, leaning in close to Reese and putting her hand on his arm. "So we only got glimpses of her face as it went around and around."

Richard glared at Kate, but she seemed totally oblivious. I started to kick her and then stopped myself. I suppose I couldn't be upset if she made a play for Reese. It wasn't like I'd ever dated him. Anyway, I'd started seeing someone. Well, I don't know if I could actually call it dating yet. But Ian, the Scottish bandleader I'd met at a wedding a couple of months ago, and I were definitely more than friends. At least I thought so.

"And that's it?" Reese asked, snapping me out of my introspection.

"As far as I can remember," I said. "Does it look like suicide or foul play?"

"Suicide?" Reese almost laughed. "Not likely."

"I told you, Annabelle," Richard said. "Carolyn wouldn't kill herself in the middle of a wedding."

"We found evidence that she didn't go down without a fight," Reese said.

"You're kidding." I shivered as I imagined Carolyn struggling with a killer.

"You're sure it isn't from Richard's fight with Giancarlo?" Kate asked, and got another dirty look from Richard.

"I'm afraid not." Reese closed his notebook and dropped it in his jacket pocket. "We found wood under her fingernails from the balcony railing and marks from where she tried to keep from being pushed over the edge."

The hairs on the back of my neck prickled. Someone had hated Carolyn Crabbe enough to drag her over the edge of the balcony, and we'd only missed walking in on it by minutes.

Chapter 6

"Well, I know what I'm getting," Kate said as we settled into a banquette at Bistro Français.

Even though it was late at night, the French bistro buzzed with activity. Waiters wearing long white aprons scuttled around the two-level mahogany and brass dining room that was almost filled to capacity. Lately it had become a habit for Kate to drag me here after we finished our Saturday wedding. She had a thing for their quiche.

"I've never been here." Fern looked around him at the stylishly dressed twenty-somethings taking a break from their late night revelry in Georgetown. "What's good?"

I picked up the menu and flipped it open. "Kate always gets the quiche Lorraine, but their fries are to die for."

"And you must try their hot chocolate," Kate added, pushing her closed menu away from her.

I let my hair down and shook it out. It had been pinned up for so long that it actually hurt.

Fern pressed a hand to his chest and sighed. "I love it when you let your hair down. You really should wear it that way more often."

"Thanks, Fern." I managed a weary smile. "I'm afraid I can't stand it getting in my face when I work, though."

Fern reached over and squeezed my hand. "But ponytails are not sexy, doll. Not the way you wear them, at least."

It would be pointless to explain to Fern that I wasn't trying to be sexy when I coordinated weddings. He and Kate came from the same school of thought: that you should always be ready to meet the man of your dreams. I found the whole concept exhausting.

Richard slumped down in the leather bench next to me. "I can't believe it's finally over. I thought we'd never get out of there."

"I still say it was awfully nice of the hotel to clear out the restaurant for us to use for the wedding." Kate slipped off her suit jacket and leaned back in her chair. "They never close down the restaurant for a private event."

I rubbed my arms to warm up and wondered how Kate didn't freeze without her jacket on. Especially considering the sleeveless dress she had on underneath. "Well, they've never had a murder in their hotel and a banquet captain who got hauled away for obstruction of justice."

Fern winked at me. "Touché."

"The bride seemed to take it all pretty well," Kate said. "She didn't even seem to notice that the bowl of honey ended up being a lot smaller than it should have been."

"It was practically a thimble," Fern said.

"She should be grateful that we emptied five hundred individual honey packets from the room service pantry for her," Richard grumbled. "It felt like I was stuck in a bad episode of *I Love Lucy*."

Fern shook his head. "Who would have guessed how many of those little packs it takes to fill a bowl?"

"The bride will never know that we had to replace the first bowl of honey because a dead woman landed in it, will she, Richard?" I said with a hint of warning in my voice.

"You wound me, Annabelle. You know I wouldn't repeat something like that," he said. "A good magician never reveals his tricks."

A waiter filled our water glasses and dropped a basket of warm bread in the center of the table. My stomach growled. I hadn't eaten a bite since I'd wolfed down half of a cinnamon scone early that morning. Luckily, I'd been too busy dealing with one wedding catastrophe after another to notice, but suddenly I was starving.

I ripped off a hot, crusty piece of bread and popped it in my mouth. "I hope the word doesn't get out about what happened. You know how these things are for business."

"I think it's safe to say everyone in town will know about it by morning," Richard said.

I put my head in my hands. "That's what I'm afraid of."

"Listen, Annie." Kate reached across the table and patted my shoulder. "You need to relax. Have you used those five weirdos that Richard gave you?"

I looked up at her. "Excuse me?"

"You know. The Guatemalan weirdos that Richard got you to help you with stress."

I almost laughed. "Do you mean the *worry dolls*?" Richard had gotten me a set of tiny worry dolls from Guatemala to place under my pillow and supposedly rid me of stress. He swore by the power of voodoo dolls, but I found them too creepy to have lying around, so he said that the worry dolls were the next best thing.

"That's what they are? I thought you guys called them weirdos." Kate reached for a piece of bread. "You have to admit, they kind of look like weirdos."

"What did I do to deserve this?" Richard muttered under his breath.

"We could call ourselves the Five Weirdos if we had one more person," Fern said.

"Leatrice would definitely qualify," Kate said, suggesting my elderly neighbor who had a fondness for off-beat clothing that made noise, covert surveillance of other neighbors in the building that bordered on stalking, and meddling in my personal life.

Fern bobbed his head. "She would make a great weirdo."

Kate nudged Fern with her elbow. "We could get special jackets made up. Leatrice would love that."

"Over my dead body." Richard folded his arms tightly in front of his chest, and Kate and Fern collapsed into fits of laughter.

"They're teasing you, Richard," I said, fighting the urge to laugh myself.

"You are both horrible people." Richard sat up very straight and turned so he faced away from Kate and Fern.

"Okay, you two." I tried to sound serious. "We really shouldn't be joking around. A woman died tonight."

Kate's face fell. "You're right. Poor Carolyn. What a way to go."

"I didn't really know her," I said. "But she was famous in the wedding industry so I knew about her."

Fern leaned over the table. "Famous and infamous."

"Meaning?" Kate nudged him. "Come on, Fern. You can't leave us hanging like that."

"When you've been planning weddings in this town as long as Carolyn Crabbe has, you make a few enemies along the way, that's all. Everyone knows that she wasn't the easiest person to work for or with."

"I can attest to the fact that she wasn't the friendliest person on the job," I said. "It's the first time another wedding planner has threatened me like that."

"To your face." Richard busily buttered a piece of bread.

I raised an eyebrow at him. "What are you saying? That people are saying things about me behind my back?"

"Of course. If you're any good in the business someone is always trying to knock you down. Carolyn had just earned her chops enough to say it to people's faces. Don't think the other planners in town aren't just as ruthless."

"Ruthless enough to kill?" I asked.

"What?" Kate said loudly, and then lowered her voice. "You think one of her competitors killed her?"

"Who else?" I said. "Unless one of her brides got really ticked off at her. Why go to the trouble of hanging her with a veil if you aren't trying to make a point?"

"Great," Kate sighed. "So that narrows the list of possible murderers."

"Yep." I leaned back and let out a long breath. "To all of our colleagues."

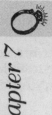

Chapter 7

"Go away," I yelled from underneath my down comforter. Someone had been knocking on my door for the past five minutes despite my best attempts to ignore them.

I poked my head out from under the covers and turned the retro metal alarm clock on my nightstand toward me. Eleven o'clock. What kind of person would bang on a wedding planner's door on a Sunday morning? Anyone who knew me knew that Sunday mornings were strictly for recuperation. I never got out of bed before noon and then only for brunch. I usually missed breakfast by hours.

Breakfast! I sat up in bed. Hadn't Ian said he would bring over bagels this morning? Since he was the lead singer of the eighties cover band The Breakfast Club and traveled most of the time, and I'd become an in-demand wedding planner who worked almost every evening and weekend, finding times to get together had proven to be tricky. I clearly had been out of my mind when I'd suggested Sunday morning, though.

The knocking continued. I leapt out of bed and pulled off the WEDDINGS ARE MURDER T-shirt I usually slept in.

"I'm coming," I yelled, pawing through my closet for something presentable. I tugged on my Seven jeans, a gift from Kate in one of her many attempts to make me more hip, and topped it with a form-fitting pink chenille sweater. I ran into the bathroom and took a swig of mouthwash and splashed cold water on my face. I spit out the mouthwash and looked at myself in the mirror.

Great. I looked exactly like I'd rolled out of bed after working for twelve hours straight on a grueling wedding. I put on some mascara and lip gloss. Not much of an improvement, but it would have to do.

I ran to the front door and threw it open in mid-apology. "I am so sorry—"

"Don't worry, dearie." My downstairs neighbor, Leatrice Butters, swept past me into the apartment, giving me the once-over as she passed. "I'm glad you're dressed already. I thought I might have woken you up."

I glared at Leatrice, who could have passed for Mary Tyler Moore if Mary had been in her eighties, under five feet, and a fan of clothes that either lit up or made noise. Today, Leatrice wore a bright yellow jogging suit and a pair of green slippers with claws that roared as she walked.

"You mean because you were pounding on my door for ten minutes?"

"Well, I knew you must be in here because you're expecting company." Leatrice glanced around my living room and craned her neck to look down the hall. "Is he here yet?"

"How did you know that Ian is coming over this morning?"

Leatrice patted her black flipped-up bob. Leatrice and Wayne Newton were the only people I knew of over sixty who had jet black hair. "He helped me hang a new shower curtain last week."

I wasn't sure how thrilled I was that Leatrice and Ian had become buddies, although I was happy that she'd found someone else to focus her attention on. I hated to think how she would take it if things didn't work out between us.

"Thanks for checking on me, Leatrice," I said through clenched teeth. "But Ian and I were kind of hoping to have some time alone."

Leatrice went over to my couch, her feet roaring as she walked, and began fluffing the pillows. "I don't plan to stay long. I came to see if you needed any help."

"Well, Ian's bringing food and I've got orange juice and coffee, so we're all set." I tapped my foot impatiently and stood holding the door open so she would get the hint.

Leatrice swept the loose papers and magazines on my coffee table into her arms. "Why don't I put on the coffee while you finish getting ready? Unless you did your hair like that on purpose. I never can tell what's fashionable with young people these days."

"Fine." I closed the door and headed back down

the hall to my bathroom. "I'll be two seconds."

"Take your time, dearie. I know my way around."

That's what I was afraid of. I brushed my hair and pulled it half up in a clip, then put on base, powder, blush, and three different shades of brown eye shadow. I hadn't put on this much makeup since my senior prom. I rubbed off some of the blush as I walked back to the kitchen.

Leatrice had indeed started boiling water for coffee and had my French press cleaned and filled with coffee grounds. She'd found two matching ceramic mugs and arranged them on a wooden tray with a couple of pale pink cocktail napkins with a former bride and groom's names imprinted in white.

"Goodness." Leatrice's eyes widened when she saw me. "I've never seen you all made up. See how lovely you can look with a little effort?"

"Thanks, Leatrice." I managed not to roll my eyes. "And for helping me get ready. I'm pretty worn-out after yesterday's catastrophe of a wedding."

"Bad bride?" she asked, taking the tray and heading out to the living room.

I hesitated to tell her about the murder since Leatrice considered herself a cross between an undercover spy and an amateur crime solver, but I knew she would find out eventually.

"I'm surprised you didn't hear about it already." I followed her roaring feet to the living room. "Don't you keep your police scanner on all the time?"

Leatrice spun around and nearly dropped the

tray. "Something happened at your wedding?"

"Don't get so excited." I took the tray from her and placed it carefully on the coffee table. "Another wedding planner was murdered. Hung with a veil, to be exact."

"What was another wedding planner doing at your wedding?"

"It's a big hotel. They can handle more than one event at a time. We wouldn't have even crossed paths if she hadn't threatened me and then ended up hanging from a balcony in our ballroom."

Leatrice perched on the edge of my couch. "So she wasn't one of the wedding planners that you're friends with?"

I gave a little laugh. "No, I wouldn't say that I was close to Carolyn Crabbe. She considered herself the Queen of Wedding Planning in D.C. and wasn't too crazy about newcomers."

"Why did she threaten you?" I could see that Leatrice fought the urge to take notes.

"Escort cards."

Leatrice's eyes widened. "Escort cards? As in escort service?" She lowered her voice. "Is this wedding planner business a cover?"

I groaned. "No, it's not what you think. Escort cards are just the cards that assign wedding guests to a table for dinner. They're nothing to get worked up about. It was her style to bully other people. I didn't take it personally."

"If she ended up murdered, it sounds like someone took something personally." Leatrice tapped her fingertips together. "Do the police think you're a suspect?"

I shook my head. "Luckily, I wasn't near the

crime scene when the murder took place, and plenty of people saw me in the hotel lobby. The fact that I found the body was purely coincidental."

"You found the body?" Leatrice's face lit up. "You really do have all the luck, dear."

Sometimes I found Leatrice's interest in real life mysteries a bit disturbing.

"I'd hardly call it lucky." I winced as I remembered Carolyn's limp body dangling from the balcony. "Creepy is more like it. I'm glad it's over and I can put the whole incident behind me."

The doorbell rang, and my heart began to pound. Leatrice leapt up and clapped her hands together.

"Don't worry, dearie, I'll make myself scarce so you two kids can finally be alone."

I smoothed my hair back and took a deep breath to steady myself before I opened the door.

It wasn't Ian. Detective Reese and another official-looking man stood on my doorstep. Both wore blazers and serious expressions.

"I'm sorry to bother you on a Sunday, Miss Archer," Reese said. "But we have a few more questions about yesterday's murder that couldn't wait."

So much for putting the whole thing behind me.

Chapter 8

"I thought you weren't a suspect," Leatrice said as I waved the two men into the room.

"She's not." Reese grinned at her and held out his hand. "It's nice to see you again."

Leatrice shook his hand but didn't return his smile. "Are you sure you aren't here for another reason?"

I groaned. I didn't like where this was headed.

Reese paused and exchanged a glance with his colleague. "Detective Hobbes will be working the case with me and wanted to ask Miss Archer about some of the other wedding planners who were at the hotel. We promise not to take up too much of your time."

Detective Hobbes looked shorter and softer around the middle than Reese. His wore his thinning ashy blond hair smoothed neatly to the side in an unmistakable comb-over. I wondered if he really thought that the style made him look like he had a full head of hair. At least he didn't wrap one long piece around his head like a braided rug. Reese's dark good looks and full head of hair stood out even more next to his pasty partner.

"Good," Leatrice said. "Because you're too late for anything else, Detective. Annabelle has been spoken for and has a date that should be arriving any minute now."

Detective Hobbes looked puzzled, but Leatrice barreled on. "You didn't expect her to wait forever, did you?"

"I'm sure that's not why the detectives are here, Leatrice." I shot her a look. "And I doubt they have any interest in my personal life. Please have a seat, guys."

Detective Hobbes sat down next to Leatrice on the couch and his eyebrows shot up when he saw her claw slippers.

She winked at him. "They roar when I walk."

Detective Reese took a seat in the armchair across from the couch and leaned forward, resting his elbows on his knees. "We'll be quick since you have a hot date." He looked at his watch. "On a Sunday morning."

I gave him my most sugary smile and sat on the arm of the couch. "You know what they say about all work and no play."

The corner of his mouth turned up in a smirk. "I'm familiar with the expression."

"You really should find yourself a nice girl, Detective." Leatrice seemed to be warming up to Reese again. "Annabelle's taken, but maybe her assistant, Kate, would be interested."

I could bet she would be. Kate was always interested.

Leatrice turned to Hobbes. "Are you married yet?"

"No," he stammered, and looked to Reese for help.

Leatrice rubbed her hands together. "Well, then. I have my work cut out for me, don't I?"

Before I could decide whether to save the detectives or not, a loud pounding came from the front door.

Leatrice jumped up and pushed by me on her way to the door. "That must be your Prince Charming, dear. Don't get up."

She threw open the door and her face fell. Richard breezed into the room past Leatrice and headed straight for the kitchen.

"If I have ever needed a drink, now is the time," he called over his shoulder. "You'll never guess where I escaped from."

I heard him pawing through my refrigerator. "I don't think I have much in there."

"What have I told you about keeping an emergency bottle of champagne, Annabelle?" I heard a gasp from the kitchen. "Please tell me this is not pink wine."

I felt my cheeks flush, and I didn't dare look at Reese. I tried to change the subject from my embarrassing fondness for girly sweet wine. "So where were you?" I asked.

"I just finished setting up a baby shower. Can you imagine me at a baby shower?"

I couldn't.

"I guess this wine will have to do," Richard sighed. "One of my best corporate clients is having a baby so I couldn't say no. The room looked stunning, of course. Butterflies everywhere. And I did a fabulous menu full of pregnancy friendly food, although it pained me not to use any brie or goat cheese whatsoever."

"That doesn't sound so bad," I said.

"Imagine not eating brie for nine months. Perish the thought." The refrigerator door opened and closed again. "Everything was fine until a few guests arrived and started talking about childbirth. I think I'm scarred for life. I mean, really. There's a reason why I don't have children."

"Only one?" I muttered, and gave Reese an apologetic smile.

"What was that, Annabelle?" Richard walked back into the living room holding a goblet full of white zinfandel in front of him. "I feel like Prissy in *Gone With the Wind*. I don't know nothing about birthing no … *Aaaah!*" He saw the two detectives and shrieked, sending his wine sloshing over his wrist.

"Don't worry, I'm not in trouble," I explained before he could bolt for the door. "They came by to ask about the other planners at the Mayflower."

Richard wiped his sleeve and nodded an acknowledgment to the detectives. He shuffled over to stand next to me and elbowed me in the ribs. "You could have told me they were here before I rambled on like that."

"I take it this isn't your date?" Reese asked with a grin.

"Oh, no." Leatrice took her seat on the couch. "These two are just friends. I gave up on them ever getting together ages ago."

"You don't say?" Reese raised an eyebrow.

"You have a date?" Richard asked, making a point to ignore Leatrice's comment. "You didn't tell me this. Do I know him?"

I turned my attention back to Detective Hobbes. "You were asking about the other planners at the Mayflower Hotel?"

Detective Hobbes produced a notepad from his pocket. "We're interested in knowing how they might have been tied to the victim. Take Byron Wolfe, for instance."

"Don't tell me you're dating Kilt Boy," Richard hissed at me.

"I saw him yesterday with Gail Gordan." I pretended not to hear Richard. "I think they do events together every so often. Their wedding wasn't at the Mayflower, though. The bride only got ready there."

Richard sucked in his breath. "You are!" he whispered. "You and I need to have a little chat, Annabelle. What have I told you about dating men who wear leather?"

"You should know," I shot back.

Detective Hobbes looked back and forth between me and Richard. "Did Byron and Gail get along with the victim?"

"Let me clarify," Richard said. "Straight men who wear leather. It's entirely different."

"He hardly ever wears leather," I said, then turned to the detective. "I didn't know them very well."

"The rest of the time he's wearing kilts and Captain America boots," Richard said. "Do I even have to mention the tattoos?"

"Tattoos aren't out of the ordinary anymore."

I pointed at my neighbor. "Leatrice almost got one."

Both detectives stared at the elderly lady.

"I changed my mind when I found out that I could only choose one picture," Leatrice said. "I like a little more variety. And they don't make noise or blink or anything."

"Can you tell us anything else about the other wedding planners?" Hobbes asked after he'd stopped staring at Leatrice.

"I can." Richard gave me a look that told me we weren't finished discussing Ian, then turned away from me and focused his attention on Detective Hobbes. "Byron is the biggest brown-noser in the business. He sucks up to all the female planners in town and they all love him. Some of them, literally."

Leatrice's eyes widened.

"What about Gail?" Reese asked.

"She's a female version of Byron," Richard said. "She's had a series of rich husbands and stays in the business as an excuse to party all the time. She's a huge gossip and one of the industry's power brokers."

"Were she and Byron involved?" I asked, and wondered why Richard had never shared this gossip before.

"There have been rumors," Richard said. "I wouldn't put it past either one of them."

The doorbell rang loudly, and I jumped up to answer the door before Leatrice could. Ian stood in the doorway in jeans and a black leather jacket. His wore his blond hair short and spiky, and his grin fell somewhere between dangerous and sexy.

My pulse quickened until I heard Richard clear his throat loudly, then I felt my cheeks flush.

Ian looked around me into the room. "Looks like you have a full house."

Leatrice joined us at the door. "Don't worry. Everyone will be leaving soon. Even me."

I knew this to be a supreme sacrifice on Leatrice's part and couldn't help smiling.

"We only have a few more questions, Annabelle, I mean Miss Archer," Reese called from inside the room.

I saw recognition cross Ian's face when he spotted Reese in my living room, and the two men nodded at each other almost imperceptibly. I couldn't help feeling awkward since I'd had feelings for both of them at one point and I think they both knew it.

Hobbes wrote furiously in his notepad without looking up. He directed his questioning to Richard. "So Gail and Byron have a lot in common, then."

Ian, standing next to me, leaned in and whispered, "It's nice to see you."

I could see Reese turn away out of the corner of my eye.

"And one other thing," Richard said. "They both started off in this industry working for Carolyn, and they both hated her with a passion."

"Why?" Hobbes and I asked simultaneously.

Richard folded his arms in front of him. "Because she ruined their lives, of course."

I gulped. Things were really starting to get interesting.

Chapter 9

"Are you sure you should have told the police gossip about Byron and Gail?" I asked Richard after the detectives had left.

"It wasn't gossip," Richard insisted. "Byron and Gail both started out working for Carolyn. It's no secret that Carolyn tried to blacklist them when they each went out on their own. Of course, Byron worked for her about ten years before Gail came along, but it's the same story for each one."

"I mean the part about them having an affair," I said, then paused. "Wait a second. Is Byron really that much older than Gail? He doesn't look it."

Richard winked at me. "Plastic surgery, darling. I said that the affair was purely speculation. No one can arrest you for sleeping around. If they could, half our industry would be in the slammer."

"At least I'd be in the clear on that one." I picked up the tray and walked to the kitchen.

Richard followed me. "I'm sorry your date fell through."

"No, you aren't. You can't stand Ian."

Richard pressed a hand against his heart in exaggerated shock. "That is not true. I merely think he isn't right for you. And he proved me right by canceling on you at the last minute."

"It wasn't his fault. They got a last minute gig at a college in North Carolina and had to drive down today." I replaced the coffee cups in the cabinets. "At least he came by to tell me in person." I pointed to a white paper bag on the counter. "And brought bagels."

"Hmmmmph." Richard didn't seem impressed. "One good thing came from it. Leatrice left."

I swatted at him. "Hey! That's not nice."

True, Leatrice had left pretty quickly after Ian did. I think she seemed more disappointed about the whole thing than me.

Richard leaned his elbows on the kitchen counter. "Are you sure you don't have a little romantic competition from your nutty neighbor?"

"I think I can handle a rivalry with an eighty-year-old who runs around in a trench coat and a fedora."

"Is she still trying to nab someone from *America's Most Wanted*?" Richard groaned.

"Do you have to ask?" I put the "Anne and Michael" cocktail napkins back on top of the stack. "And now she watches *Cops*, too. I hear her singing the theme song in the hall all the time."

"At least that gives you fair warning that she's coming."

"That and her battery operated clothing," I said. "We should be grateful that she didn't want to stay and discuss the murder."

"What's to discuss?" Richard took the last swig of his wine. "I, for one, don't want to relive the horror any more than I have to."

I felt wobbly in the knees thinking about Carolyn's lifeless body swinging in midair. "You don't think Byron or Gail really had anything to do with the murder, do you?"

"I know neither one ended things on good terms with Carolyn, but a lot of people had issues with her. I don't think that's a reason to kill someone."

I shook my head. "People have killed over a lot less."

"What would Gail or Byron gain from Carolyn's death?" Richard rinsed out his wineglass and pulled down a paper towel to dry it. "That's a lot of effort to go to just to get back at someone."

"You're right, but then who killed her?"

"That's for the police to find out, Annabelle." Richard eyed me. "If you're thinking of getting any more involved in this mess than we already are, you've lost your mind."

I waved off his concern. "Don't worry. You don't have to tell me twice."

"Oh, I think I do. Do I need to remind you what happened the last time I warned you not to stick your nose in police business?"

"I was a different person then."

"Two months ago?"

"My point is that I have no intention of investigating the death of Carolyn Crabbe. Detective Reese and his pudgy pal can have that all to themselves."

Richard put the back of his hand to his forehead. "You don't know how relieved I am to hear you say that."

"I can't promise not to talk about it, though. I'm sure everyone will be asking about it at the Organization of Wedding Planners meeting tomorrow."

Richard rubbed his temples. "You have an OWP meeting tomorrow?"

"At the Willard. All the wedding planners in town will be there, including lots of the old-timers who know the scoop on Carolyn and her possible enemies. I'm dying to find out all the people who had it in for Carolyn."

"Be careful, Annabelle. The guest list could very well include a killer."

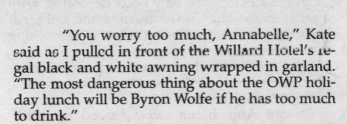

Chapter 10

"You worry too much, Annabelle," Kate said as I pulled in front of the Willard Hotel's regal black and white awning wrapped in garland. "The most dangerous thing about the OWP holiday lunch will be Byron Wolfe if he has too much to drink."

"I don't know why we have booze at a lunch meeting anyway. It isn't even noon."

"If you ask me, it takes the edge off everyone." Kate opened the passenger side door as I rolled to a stop and stepped out of the car. "Not a bad idea with this crowd."

I handed my keys to the approaching valet. "To have them drink too much and get sloppy?"

"No." Kate grinned at me. "It takes the edge off them if *I* drink."

I raised an eyebrow and led the way up the stairs and through the revolving brass door into the hotel lobby. To call the Willard lobby ornate would be an understatement. Enormous marble

columns rose two stories in the air and a massive
Christmas tree stood in the center of the lobby
surrounded by wrapped boxes. Poinsettia trees in
colorful Chinese planters were dotted throughout
the room, making the lobby a riot of red. Some
of the usual furniture had been moved to accom-
modate a life-sized gingerbread sleigh filled with
presents and surrounded by fake snow. I took a
deep breath and inhaled the sugary aroma of the
royal icing that held the sleigh together.

"We're in the Crystal Room." Kate motioned
toward the long corridor on the other side of the
lobby. Peacock Alley had been decorated with
a series of frosted Christmas trees and tall birch
branches that made it feel like we were walking
through a forest.

"Well, if it isn't the two cutest little wedding
planners in the city." The nasal voice and sarcastic
tone made my skin crawl.

Eleanor Applebaum stood behind the OWP
registration desk outside the doors to the Crystal
Room wearing a forest green polyester suit and a
laminated name tag. Her mousy brown hair fell to
her shoulders, and she sported feathered bangs.
Eleanor had apparently stopped reading fashion
magazines in the mid–eighties.

I forced a smile. "Hi, Eleanor. How are you?"

"Insanely busy, of course." Eleanor gave us her
best fake smile as looked us up and down. "I have
so many brides that I can barely see straight. I really shouldn't be here today."

"Don't let us keep you here, then." Kate returned the smile as she found our name tags on
the table and handed mine to me.

Eleanor's smile faltered for a moment. "Too bad about your recent run of bad luck with weddings. Maybe there are a few brides who haven't heard about it."

"You mean the bad luck of having a wedding featured in the hottest wedding magazine around?" Fern walked up behind us and linked his arms through ours. "Let's go get a drink, girls."

Eleanor pressed her lips into a white line as Fern led us from the registration table to the bar a few feet away at the base of a long set of wide red carpeted stairs.

"What are you doing here?" Kate asked after ordering a glass of white wine. "Not that we don't owe you for saving us from Eleanor."

"Don't even give her a second thought. She blows more hot air than my hair dryer." Fern didn't bother to lower his voice. "I'm doing the program for your meeting today, remember? The newest trends in bridal beauty from Washington's most deluxe hairstylist."

"Of course." I ordered a Coke from the bartender. "Are you ready?"

"My equipment is all set up in the Crystal Room. Now I need my model." Fern glanced at his jewel-encrusted watch. "She should have been here by now. I'm going to run and check the lobby again."

I took my Coke from the bartender and sized up the crowd as Fern pushed his way through it. Lots of wedding planners of all ages were milling around in Peacock Alley holding glasses of wine. It looked like I was the only person not drinking today. I took a sip of my Coke. I knew I had to be on my toes with this bunch.

"Feeling lucky?"

"What?" I was pulled from my thoughts by the perky voice of Stephanie Burke.

"Do you want to buy a raffle ticket?" Stephanie asked, holding a roll of red tickets in front of me. "The money goes to our charity."

Stephanie was one of the newest members of OWP and also one of the newest wedding planners in town. She had curly dark hair that she wore loose down her back and brightly lacquered pink nails. She'd gotten roped into being the OWP recruiting director almost as soon as she'd joined because she was bouncy and energetic and had no idea what a crappy job it was.

"What's our charity?" Kate asked.

Stephanie blinked a few times. "Something about helping indigent wedding planners, I think."

"There are indigent wedding planners?" Kate looked concerned and began digging in her purse.

I tugged on Kate's sleeve once she had purchased a raffle ticket and Stephanie moved on. "Look over there. Byron and Gail."

They were deep in conversation by the door to the Crystal Room, but it didn't look friendly. Byron held Gail by the elbow until Gail wrenched her arm free and stalked away, leaving Byron red-faced and fuming by himself.

"I wonder what that's all about," Kate said.

"Lover's quarrel?"

"Doubtful." Kate shook her head. "I don't get

the vibe from them. I wouldn't be surprised if they were involved at one point, but not anymore."

I usually trusted Kate's instincts when it came to men and dating.

"Don't look now, but here comes Botox Barbie." Kate downed her wine as Barbie Sitwell advanced on us, her collagen lips arriving well before the rest of her face. She'd teased her hair high off her forehead and gone about three shades blonder since the last time I'd seen her.

"Annabelle, Kate." She gave air kisses all around. "I was so distressed to hear about what happened at your wedding. And about Carolyn, of course. You know I had my third wedding at the Mayflower."

I'd never been able to determine how many times Barbie had been married, but I suspected she could keep her business afloat by planning her own weddings.

"It was pretty awful," Kate said.

Barbie pulled us close to her in a huddle. "I heard she was hanging by a veil."

"I don't know if we should talk about it," I said.

"I would never have mentioned it if Margery and Lucille hadn't told me about it first." Barbie put a finger to her lips. "You know I despise gossip."

About as much as she despised cute pool boys and alimony payments.

"Lucille and Margery are here?" I looked around the hallway. "I'm surprised they felt good enough to come today."

"They're a bit of a mess, actually." Barbie looked

behind her as she spoke. "They didn't know if they were going to stay for the whole meeting. Not that I blame them."

"Lucille didn't take Carolyn's death too well," I said.

Barbie touched a hand to her shellacked hair. "She's always been sensitive. I've heard she cries every time someone cancels their wedding."

"We never get emotionally attached to our brides," Kate said. "Probably because they're all insane."

I glared at Kate. "She's kidding."

"You don't have to apologize to me." Barbie giggled. "I know exactly what you mean. Even I've been known to turn into Bridezilla from time to time."

"Isn't that the truth," Gail Gordan said as she joined our conversation. Gail wore her dark hair in a French twist and rarely had a hair out of place. "Don't forget that I coordinated your last wedding."

Barbie threw her arm around Gail's shoulder. "Who better to plan a wedding planner's wedding than the OWP president herself?"

Gail had managed to be president of the organization more times than anyone on record. No one else had been able to take the internal politics and back-stabbing for more than a year without having a meltdown. Gail survived mainly because she was responsible for most of the internal politics and back-stabbing.

"Great place for the holiday lunch, Gail," I said.

"Isn't it?" She gestured at the brightly decorated

trees around us. "No one can touch the Willard's Christmas decor."

"Too bad we didn't get to chat more at the Mayflower on Saturday," I said. "You and Byron seemed really busy."

"Byron was a lifesaver." Gail's cheeks reddened. "We were trying to get our bride over to St. Matthew's Cathedral on time. You know how the monsignor there can be."

"So you both left with the bride for the church?" I asked.

"Pretty much." Gail's eyes didn't meet mine. "I got in the limo with the bridal party, and Byron walked over since there wasn't room."

"Too bad you missed all the drama at the hotel," Kate said.

Gail bit her lower lip. "Will you excuse me a moment? It looks like our registration desk needs help."

"Don't take it personally," Barbie whispered. "She avoids any mention of Carolyn since they had that falling out when they worked together and Carolyn fired her."

"When was that?" I asked.

Barbie tapped her chin. "About ten years ago, I guess."

Kate's eyes widened. "And she still can't talk about her?"

"It's been a long healing process." Barbie drained her wineglass and looked toward the bar. "Does anyone else need another drink?"

We shook our heads as Barbie teetered off, passing a highly agitated Fern heading straight for us.

"This is a disaster," he said when he reached us. "My model is a no-show."

"Are you sure?" I asked.

"Well, we start in five minutes and she's no-where to be found." Fern wrung his hands. "I'm going to look like a fool in front of every wedding planner in town."

Kate patted his arm. "Can we do anything?"

"Since you asked, I did have an idea." Fern gave us his most ingratiating smiles.

I began to shake my head. "Please tell me it isn't what I think it is."

"You must admit, you'd make a perfect example of a 'before' look, Annabelle." Fern took us by the elbows and propelled us through the crowd.

I sighed. "Promise me you won't give me a bee-hive."

"And no cutting," Kate warned.

Fern held up a hand as we reached the door of the Crystal Room. "Scouts' honor. You won't regret this, girls. Trust me."

Fern pulled open the door and we slipped inside the dimly lit room. With only the light coming through the windows on the opposite wall, the towering pale green marble columns that dominated the room gave an almost eerie glow. Round tables draped in gold cloths took up most of the room except for a space at the front that had been set up with a riser and podium.

"My table is already in place." Fern led us through the tables toward the riser. "I came early and put all my equipment out so I'd be ready to go as soon as people sat down for lunch. I want to dazzle everyone before they get too involved in their salads."

"Good thinking," Kate said. "Strike while the iron is not."

"Exactly," Fern said.

I shook my head and decided not to correct them.

"What is this?" Fern shrieked as he got closer to the front. "My table is a mess."

He ran the last few steps and stopped short when he reached the riser. He clamped his hands over his mouth. I stepped around him and Kate to get a better look, and I froze when I saw what they were both staring at.

Eleanor Applebaum lay sprawled facedown on the riser with what looked like the cord of a curling iron wrapped around her neck.

This wasn't looking like a good week to be a wedding planner.

Chapter 11

"My God!" I said, taking a step closer to the body.

"My curling iron!" Fern motioned to the chrome wand hanging down the back of Eleanor's neck.

Kate and I turned to look at Fern.

"Does this make me an accomplice?" he asked.

I put a hand on his shoulder. "I don't think you can be held accountable for someone using your curling iron to strangle her."

Fern made a tiny noise in the back of his throat and sunk into the nearest chair. "This is horrible."

I agreed. Eleanor's lifeless body sprawled across the riser, her arms and legs jutting out at unnatural angles. Bright red marks slashed her throat and the cord was still wound loosely around her neck.

Kate darted a glance at the body. "I don't suppose she decided to end it all in a really dramatic way."

"Doubtful," I said. "Someone took a big chance murdering her with all these people around."

"Maybe she ticked off someone and they killed her in the heat of passion," Kate suggested. "Eleanor could be really annoying with all her competitive bragging and snide comments."

Fern nodded. "If I heard her talking one more time about all the celebrity weddings she did, I might have killed her myself."

"No kidding," Kate said. "Maybe someone finally snapped, having to hear about her million dollar weddings for the hundredth time."

"Don't say that too loudly," I warned, looking back at the door.

Fern grinned. "If only someone had told her that hosting a cable access cooking show does not make someone a celebrity. It would have saved us all a lot of pain and suffering."

"You two are awful." I folded my arms in front of me. "The woman is dead and you're making fun of her."

"Well, I made fun of her when she was alive," Fern said. "I don't want to be a hypocrite."

Great. Now he'd decided to take an ethical stand.

"Let's get serious, you two." I leveled a finger at Kate and Fern. "We have close to fifty wedding planners who are going to walk in this room any second and find us with Eleanor."

"You're right," Kate said. "This doesn't look so great. Especially since we found Carolyn a couple of days ago in a similar state."

"Exactly." I didn't want to think about what Detective Reese would say. "The police aren't going to be thrilled with us, that's for sure."

"But it's a case of being in the wrong place at the wrong time," Kate insisted. "We've just had really bad luck."

"I'm not so sure about that anymore," I said.

Fern studied me for a moment. "What do you mean?"

"Don't you think it's an awfully big coincidence that two of our competitors are killed almost right in front of us?"

Fern looked thoroughly confused. "Is this your way of telling us that you did it?"

"No." I glared at him. "What if we're being set up?"

Kate's mouth fell open. "You mean the real killer wants it to look like we're killing our fellow planners?"

"Maybe," I said. "I don't know for sure. I'm just trying to make sense of it all."

"But why?" Fern wrung his hands. "Everyone loves me."

"You could be right, Annabelle," Kate said. "I wouldn't be surprised if some of the planners who've been doing this forever were threatened by how fast we've been rising in the ranks."

Fern held up his hands. "Let me see if I understand correctly. Some of the established wedding planners get upset that a couple of upstart hussies are taking their business so they start to kill each other?"

"Upstart hussies?" I tapped my foot on the floor.

"I'm trying to get inside the mind of a killer, Annabelle. Don't take it personally."

Somehow I didn't think that a cold-blooded killer would use the term "upstart hussies," but I didn't want to debate the point.

Kate tapped her chin. "He has a point. Why would they kill other old school planners? Why not just kill us?"

I swallowed hard. "Maybe they plan to kill us, too."

"Whoa, whoa, whoa." Fern stood and put his hands on his hips. "This isn't funny. I don't want to be found with a blow dryer cord around my neck."

"Do you suspect anyone in particular?" Kate asked.

"Aside from everyone in the hall?" I nibbled on my lower lip. "I think we have to assume that any of our colleagues could be the killer."

Fern sat back down again and fanned himself with his hand. "I don't know if I can deal with this stress. It's very bad for my complexion."

I took a deep breath and looked back and forth between Kate and Fern. "We have to find out who's been murdering D.C.'s wedding planners before they get to us."

Chapter 12

"We're goners," Fern whispered to me as all the guests from the OWP meeting were corralled into the Willard's 1401 Café across from the Crystal Room. The modern café looked completely different from the rest of the ornate hotel. Instead of marble, it featured plenty of sleek blond wood and glass.

"Don't panic," I said. "The police want to keep us all in one place until they can question everyone."

Fern led us to a small table near the back of the café. "Don't you mean they've trapped us with a murderer?"

Kate angled her chair so her back faced the wall. "We'd better lay on our toes unless we want to be next."

Fern gave evil glances to everyone around him.

"Calm down, you two," I said. "Nobody is going to try anything with an officer stationed at the door and dozens of witnesses. Not that it would hurt to *stay* on our toes."

Fern visibly relaxed and squeezed my hand. "Of course you're right. I'm just so upset that someone was murdered with my equipment. I don't even know if they make that curling iron anymore."

"It's probably still usable," Kate said.

Fern's mouth gaped open. "I hope you're not suggesting I use a murder weapon to style my brides' hair."

Kate rested her arms on the table. "It's not like your brides would ever know. There wasn't any blood on it or anything."

The color left Fern's face at the mention of blood, and he slumped onto the table. "I don't feel so good."

"It's evidence anyway," I reminded them. "You probably won't see it for a while."

"Is it true?" Barbie slid her chair over next to mine. "Did you find Eleanor?"

"I'm afraid so," I said, hoping that my terse answer would discourage her. Fat chance.

"I can't believe it." Barbie shook her head and came as close to a frown as a person with all of their facial muscles deadened could. "She just told me about a huge wedding she was working on. Apparently for some Middle Eastern princess."

Fern looked up and raised an eyebrow. "What did I tell you? This wasn't a murder. It was a justifiable homicide."

"What?" Barbie perked up.

I shot daggers at Fern. "He's joking. Gallows humor, you know."

"Oh." Barbie looked deflated. "You're the hairdresser, aren't you?"

Fern sat up and threw his shoulders back. "Fern at your service."

"Like the plant?"

Fern gave her a withering look. "It's short for Fernando. My mother was an Abba groupie."

Kate almost slipped off her chair. "Really?"

Fern pressed a hand to his heart and sucked in air. "Did you think I was named after a house plant?"

Kate shook her head and spluttered. "Of course not."

"Well, of all the ridiculous things." Fern crossed his arms tightly in front of him and spun around in his chair so his back was to us.

Barbie hesitated as she turned her attention back to me. "I can't imagine who would have done this to her, can you?"

"Did you see Eleanor talking with anyone suspicious?" Kate asked, trying to avoid Fern's over the shoulder glares.

Barbie shook her head. "She manned the registration desk. She had to talk to everyone."

"Right." Kate leaned back in her chair. "So much for narrowing down the field."

Barbie's eyes widened. "Are you trying to figure out who killed her?"

"No," I said, perhaps a bit too forcefully. "We're not getting involved in this at all. Are we, Kate?"

Kate took my cue. "Absolutely not. We always let the police do their job."

Luckily, Barbie didn't catch Kate's sarcasm or me kicking her under the table.

Gail walked over and sat in the empty chair next to Fern. Her usual reelection smile had vanished. "The police are ruining our holiday meeting."

"I think the fact that one of our members was murdered actually ruined the meeting," Kate said.

Gail ignored her and turned to me. "How much longer do you think this will take?"

Since when did I become the expert in police protocol? "As long as it takes to question everyone, I guess."

Gail threw her hands in the air. "That could take all day. This is a disaster. One member dead, two taken away for grief counseling, and the rest of us stuffed like sardines in this restaurant."

"Who got taken away for grief counseling?" I asked.

"Lucille and Margery," Barbie jumped in before Gail could respond. "Apparently Eleanor's death pushed Lucille over the edge. The police brought in a grief counselor, and Margery went with her to make sure she'd be okay."

I felt sorry for Lucille. She'd never been the toughest planner around, which I guessed was why she'd remained an assistant for so many years. At least she still had Margery for support.

"Well, I have an important meeting this afternoon," Gail said. "I can't afford to sit around here twiddling my thumbs all day." She stood up. "I'm going to go talk to the police and see if I can't speed things up."

The uniformed officer who'd been guarding the door approached our table. "They'd like to see you now, Miss Archer."

I motioned to Kate and Fern. "Only me?"

Gail opened and closed her mouth a few times before stalking off. I followed the officer out of the café and across Peacock Alley to the Crystal Room.

The ballroom that had previously been so calm and serene now buzzed with activity. Light filled the room and officers swarmed around the riser at the front. I walked to where Detectives Reese and Hobbes stood facing the body. I couldn't help notice how Reese's dark green sweater fit snugly over his broad back and tapered to his narrow waist. There was no such tapering for Hobbes, whose own striped sweater looked a little lumpy around the middle.

I cleared my throat, and Reese turned around.

"Good, you're here." He took my arm and led me to one of the nearby tables. "I wanted to talk to you privately before you're questioned."

I couldn't help feeling pleased as I sat down and folded my hands in my lap. I gave Reese a weak smile. "I know you're probably really upset that I found another body."

Reese arched an eyebrow, and I noticed how green his eyes looked against his sweater. "Why would that upset me?"

"I swear I had nothing to do with it. I was in the wrong place at the wrong time."

Reese held up a hand to stop me. "I don't think you killed her, Annabelle."

I let out a long sigh. "That's a relief."

"I don't know if you should be so relieved," he continued. "These aren't just two unrelated murders you happened onto."

I swallowed hard. He confirmed my worst suspicions. "You think they're connected?"

Reese gave a curt nod. "The murders have the same M.O.'s. It's pretty clear that we're looking for a single killer for both murders."

I took a shaky breath as his words sunk in.

Reese placed his hand over mine, and I felt the warmth spread up my arm. "You need to watch your back, Annabelle. We may have a serial killer on the loose. And one of the things that connects both of the deaths is you."

Chapter 13

"What about the rest of us?" Richard's voice crackled through my cell phone.

"You're upset that two murders aren't linked to you as well?" I rubbed my temples and ducked behind a mannequin wearing a pink cocktail-length bridesmaid's dress.

Kate and I were meeting a bride and her mother at Promise bridal salon for the final fitting, and we'd arrived early. The bright and cheery salon had glass walls on two sides overlooking busy Wisconsin Avenue, one of the arteries that ran straight through the city. A wall of white billowing wedding gowns lined a back wall, and some of the most dramatic dresses stood on mannequins in the windows. Glass display cases held an impressive array of jeweled tiaras, feathered combs, and designer bridal shoes. There was even a display of trendy bridesmaids' gifts ranging from monogrammed makeup bags to preppy totes.

"Don't be absurd," Richard said. "I just don't

know why they think the only common element in both deaths is you. You didn't find the bodies alone."

"I'm not the only link. They warned Kate, too. She was there both times as well." I sighed. "I promise never to stumble onto another corpse without you."

"At least you could have called me immediately. I had to hear it from our secretary who heard it from Gail's assistant."

"Gail has an assistant? I thought she used Byron as her assistant."

"You're missing my point, Annabelle."

"Fine. I'm sorry I didn't let you know right away. It won't happen again."

Richard sniffed. "Apology accepted. I'm only concerned about your well-being, you know."

"You hate getting scooped."

"You wound me, darling. After all the sacrifices I've made for you."

I rolled my eyes. I could imagine the manufactured tears welling up in his eyes. "Oh, jeez."

"Did you roll your eyes at me?"

"Here they come," Kate called from across the salon. I looked out the glassed front of the salon and saw a pair of petite blondes approaching in long caramel-colored fur coats.

"I have to go, Richard. Are we still on for dinner tonight?"

"Well, I suppose so. But if you stumble onto another violent crime and get so busy that you forget to call me, don't worry. I'll understand." If he got any more dramatic he'd have to get a slot on late night TV.

"I'll see you then." I flipped my phone shut and dropped it in my purse as the glass doors opened and Lady Margaret and Kitty Winchester made their entrance.

Lady Margaret Winchester and her mother, Kitty, were from Dallas and looked every bit the part. They had matching blond, bouffant hairdos that a wind tunnel wouldn't budge and perfectly applied makeup. They were the only people I knew who would dare to wear real fur in such a politically correct city.

Kate rushed forward to greet them, and I prayed that she wouldn't curtsy. It had taken a bit of convincing for Kate to believe that "Lady" wasn't a title but a first name not uncommon in the South. I had to agree, though, if there was American royalty, the Dallas born and bred Winchesters would be it.

"Do forgive us for being late." Kitty's voice dripped slow and thick like molasses as she handed her coat to Kate. She wore a stunning blue suit that probably cost more than I made in a month, and her ears glittered with enormous sapphire and diamond earrings. "I hope you weren't waiting too long."

"Not at all," I said. I stepped forward to help Kate with the mound of fur draped over her. I took one of the coats and hung it on the coatrack by the door as Jessica, the stylish young salon owner, appeared. Jessica wore a fuchsia dress with a narrow belt and a knee-length bell skirt that looked remarkably like one of the bridesmaids' dresses from their casual collection.

"I apologize for my delay," Fern called out as

he burst inside the salon along with a blast of frigid air.

Lady's face lit up. "We didn't know you were coming."

Fern tossed his long black coat on top of Kate and linked his arm through the bride's. "I never miss a fitting, sweetie. I help with the whole look, you know. The hair is just the finishing touch." He turned to Kitty and winked at her. "Is that an Escada suit?"

"Why don't we see the dress?" Jessica gestured to the back of the salon. "You're going to be thrilled with the alterations."

Fern picked up a feathered hair comb from a glass display as he followed Jessica and Lady to the back. "Have you considered wearing feathers with your tiara?"

I made a mental note to restrain Fern from outfitting Lady in a feather headdress before the fitting was over.

"Now, Annabelle ...," Kitty held my arms so that Lady walked out of earshot. Her forehead furrowed into rows of wrinkles. "I need your advice."

"I promise he'll be perfectly appropriate on the wedding day."

"I'm not worried about Fern." Kitty gave a wave of her hand and smiled. "We're having some problems with the groom's side."

I nodded solemnly. Problems with the groom's family were nothing new with this wedding. I'd finally convinced Kitty that she couldn't do anything about the groom's mother selecting a hot pink fringed gown to wear to the wedding, but I knew it was killing her inside. I hoped she didn't want to rehash Gowngate again.

"You know that some of the groom's family is coming over from Ireland." She waited for me to nod before she continued. "I'm concerned that they might get intoxicated at the wedding."

Might? I didn't know how to respond. The Irish weddings I'd planned were some of the wildest parties I'd ever attended, with guests dancing and singing until the wee hours. I suspected that had something to do with the fact that they were usually drunk before the ceremony even began.

"You see, many of the guests are from our church in Dallas and they don't drink at all," Kitty continued. "Do you think there is a way to keep the drinking under control?"

Not invite the Irish guests, I felt like saying. Instead I plastered a big smile on my face. "We could have a separate nonalcoholic bar with some fun drinks like flavored tonics and lemonades. We can pass them out as well. That way people are encouraged to take something nonalcoholic instead of going to the bar."

"Great idea," Kitty said. "Let's do that."

I knew the reality was that guests who wanted a drink would find the bar no matter what we did. We could have showgirls passing out lemonade and that still wouldn't make it more appealing to people who wanted a real drink. Of course if alcohol was a problem, I suspected showgirls weren't on the approved list, either.

Kitty and I continued to the back of the salon, where Lady stood on a round platform in her wedding dress, looking at her reflection from all angles in the ornately carved wall-sized mirrors. Fern knelt on the ground next to her, fussing with the veil.

Kitty pressed her hands to her cheeks. "You look more beautiful than you did the night you won the Miss Dallas pageant."

Lady beamed. The ivory satin ball gown had a heavily beaded strapless bodice and a champagne-colored sash that cinched the waist and draped down the back of the cathedral-length train. A sparkling diamond necklace, which I didn't doubt was real, rested on Lady's exposed neckline. With her pageant hair and picture-perfect smile, she did look like she could have stepped off a Miss America runway.

"It's a French bustle." Jessica poked her head from behind the dress, where she held up the skirt.

"Will you number or color code the ribbons?" Kate asked. She'd been as scarred as I'd been a few years ago when a bridal salon had forgotten to number the strings that we were supposed to match up and tie underneath a gown in order to bustle it. We'd finally resorted to using dozens of safety pins to make the bustle work, and neither of us wanted to do that again.

Jessica smiled. "We'll number them."

Fern stood and put a hand on his hip. "Is there any way to get a longer veil? This barely extends past the train. I've had longer bathrobes."

"We do have a longer one in stock," Jessica said. "Are you sure you want one so long?"

"Oh, yes." Lady beamed at Fern. "That's exactly what the dress needs."

Jessica disappeared in the back and came back with another veil. Fern pulled the old one out of Lady's hair and slid the new veil in, then ran around behind her to unfurl it.

He clapped his hands together. "Perfect."

Lady nodded. "How to I keep the veil out of my face?" She pushed the frothy white tulle behind her shoulders, and it fell forward again.

Jessica produced a blue spray bottle from behind a display case. "Hair spray." She held the veil off Lady's face and sprayed a fine mist over the transparent fabric, then waited a few seconds for it to set before letting it go.

Lady moved her head and the veil stayed in place. "Amazing!" She turned to me to say something, but I anticipated her question.

"Don't worry, Lady. We always have hair spray with us," I assured her.

Jessica gave me a conspiratorial smile. A bridal salon had to have almost as many tricks to fix bridal mishaps as a wedding coordinator, and I'd gotten some of my best quick fixes by watching the dress consultants at Promise.

Lady spun around on the platform and blinked away tears. "I can't believe I'm getting married this Saturday."

"Don't ruin your makeup, sugar," Kitty said. "We have a luncheon after this."

Lady gave herself one more blinding smile in the mirror before stepping down and swirling into the dressing room. "Remind me to pick up the white fox stole from Neimans, Mother. Otherwise I'll freeze getting from the Bentley to the church."

Leave it to a Dallas bride to wear a fur coat to her wedding.

Kitty turned to me once Lady had disappeared into the dressing room. "Now, don't forget that we have two boxes of Devil Pickles being shipped to you for the welcome baskets."

How could I forget that they were doing themed welcome baskets with only items from Texas? I'd had boxes from the Lone Star State arriving at my apartment for a month.

"What about the guest book and pillow?" Lady called from behind the purple velvet dressing room curtain.

"Would you girls do me a huge favor?" Kitty pulled a platinum credit card from her purse. "I'm afraid we won't have time to buy a guest book and ring bearer's pillow. Could you get them for us?"

"You want me to take your credit card?" I hesitated as she held the card in front of me.

"Don't worry." She pressed it in my hand and winked at me. "I've got lots more."

"It would be our pleasure," I said as Kate gaped at me. Only days ago I'd sworn that I would not get suckered into running errands for clients, and especially not the bizarre ones that Lady and Kitty had come up with over the past few months. Kate and I had already spent an afternoon picking out a selection of wedding lingerie for Lady to approve, and then another day trying to return what she didn't like.

"You're a doll." Kitty walked to the front of the salon and threw her fur coat around her shoulders. "Remember that Lady loves beads and crystals. Something to coordinate with her dress would be perfect."

"Do we need another trail for my hair?" Lady asked Fern, coming up behind us and pulling her coat off the stand.

Fern gave a quick shake of his head. "Don't you worry. I know you Texas girls like it full."

Lady smiled and turned to her mother. "Are we all set?"

"The girls are going to take care of everything for us." Kitty patted me and Kate on the arm as she opened the glass door. "I don't know what we'd do without you two."

Kitty and Lady waved as they rushed out into the biting wind.

"How much fuller can her hair get?" I asked without breaking my smile.

Fern laughed. "The higher the hair, the closer to God."

"This isn't your first Texas bride, is it?" I asked.

"Not by a long shot." He sighed.

Kate glared at me. "What just happened with Kitty? What happened to standing your mound?"

Fern scratched his head. "I've never heard that one before."

"Okay, so I have a hard time saying no to Kitty. I think it's the accent," I said. "But I also had an ulterior motive."

Kate crossed her arms in front of her. "You're dying to check out the latest styles in ring bearer pillows?"

"No. I thought it would be a great excuse to visit the Wedding Shoppe."

"You mean Carolyn's Wedding Shoppe? Where Margery and Lucille work?"

"Exactly," I said. "We can ask a few questions and maybe find out a little more about Carolyn and who would want to kill her."

"Not a bad idea," Kate admitted. "Anything to bring us closer to finding who has it in for wedding planners. I'm afraid the next victim might be someone I actually like."

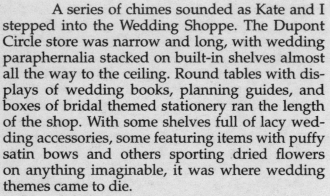

Chapter 14

A series of chimes sounded as Kate and I stepped into the Wedding Shoppe. The Dupont Circle store was narrow and long, with wedding paraphernalia stacked on built-in shelves almost all the way to the ceiling. Round tables with displays of wedding books, planning guides, and boxes of bridal themed stationery ran the length of the shop. With some shelves full of lacy wedding accessories, some featuring items with puffy satin bows and others sporting dried flowers on anything imaginable, it was where wedding themes came to die.

"Can I help you?" A thin twenty-something woman with short dark hair approached us. "Are both of you brides?"

Kate gave an involuntary gasp. Despite her chosen profession, she wasn't in any hurry to walk down the aisle herself. I think she realized that marriage would put a damper on her active dating life.

"Actually, neither of us are brides," I said. "We're wedding planners."

The woman's smile faltered. I guess the competition didn't stop by too often.

"We're looking for a ring bearer's pillow and a guest book." Kate scanned the shelves. "Something in off-white with beads."

"No problem." The woman rallied her selling skills and led us to a shelf that featured wedding items covered in lace and seed pearls. "This is the Venetian collection. It's very popular with our traditional brides."

I studied the display and frowned. "I think our client wants something with a little more flash."

"Flash?" The woman ran her eyes up and down the shelves, then led us back to the front of the store and climbed on a sliding step ladder to reach a top shelf. She pulled down a small pillow delicately embroidered with iridescent beads and ribbon. "How about the Parisian collection?"

Kate looked at me and shook her head. "Not enough glitz," she called up to the saleswoman.

"Really?" She stepped down and put her hands on her hips as she looked around at the various displays. "More glitz than the Venetian or Parisian?"

"I probably should mention that the bride is from Texas," I said. "Actually, she was Miss Texas."

The woman's face relaxed into a wide smile. "Why didn't you say that in the first place? Come with me."

We followed her to the very back of the store, where she pulled a heavily beaded oversized ring bearer's pillow off the shelf. "The Liberace collection. It's very popular with brides from Texas."

Kate took it from her and inspected it. "I'm guessing there's a pillow somewhere under the beads."

"It's perfect," I said. "Do you have a matching guest book?"

"Of course." The sales clerk produced a glittery book from the shelf. The bugle beads dangling off the wide cover made it the noisiest guest book I'd seen. Not to mention the largest. I could see why it was so popular with the Texas crowd.

"We'll take them both." I produced Kitty's credit card and handed it over.

"Annabelle? Kate?" Lucille's warbling voice came from the door leading to the back of the shop. "Is that really you?"

"I'm surprised she's working," Kate said to me in a low voice. "Shouldn't she be in grief counseling or something?"

"That's what I said," the sales clerk mumbled as she walked past us on the way to the cash register up front.

Lucille came toward us wearing a colorful Christmas sweater. With her snow white hair she would have looked remarkably like Mrs. Claus if it hadn't been for her red, swollen eyes. "It's good of you to come. Margery and I didn't think we'd see anyone before the viewing on Thursday."

"We wanted to see how you two are holding up." Kate patted Lucille on the arm. If I didn't know better I'd have thought she sounded sincere.

Lucille sniffled. "It's hard to go on without her. The shop isn't the same."

I nodded, even though this was the first time I'd actually set foot in the Wedding Shoppe. My only interaction with Carolyn Crabbe hadn't been a particularly pleasant one, so I had a hard time imagining her bringing sunshine to the workplace.

"At least you have good help." I motioned to the sales clerk ringing up our purchases.

"Dora is wonderful, but she's the only sales associate we have left." Lucille shook her head. "Carolyn had to let two longtime employees go last week, so now we're very short-staffed."

"She probably didn't plan on getting murdered when she fired them," Kate said.

Lucille dissolved into tears, and I glared at Kate. *Nice going,* I mouthed.

"Lucille." Margery appeared behind her in a conservative beige tweed suit. It seemed like everything she wore was a shade of brown. "You're in no state to be on the sales floor."

"You're right." Lucille wiped away her tears. "Please excuse me, girls."

"I'm sorry if we upset her," I said once Lucille had disappeared into the back of the store.

"It's not your fault." Margery gave a wave of her hand. "She's always been the emotional one. She cries every time she hears Pachelbel's Canon, and you know how many brides use that for a processional song. She's been hysterical since she saw Carolyn's body, though. Yesterday didn't help matters, either."

"Wasn't it awful about Eleanor?" I shook my head. "The second dead wedding planner must have sent Lucille over the edge."

Margery looked over her shoulder toward the back of the shop. "Two dead planners and two dead bosses."

"Pardon?" I tried to keep the surprise out of my voice.

"You knew that Eleanor was Carolyn's original business partner, didn't you?" Margery said. "Of course that was ages ago. Lucille and I had just started working for them when she and Carolyn split."

"Was it a friendly split?" Kate asked.

Margery raised an eyebrow. "You really didn't know Carolyn, did you? Even back then Eleanor wasn't very sophisticated, but she was a whiz at paperwork. Carolyn used her to get the business set up but then dumped her once the company started getting high-end weddings."

I gave a low whistle. "That explains Eleanor's obsession with celebrity weddings. She must have been trying to compete with Carolyn."

Margery nodded. "Even though Carolyn dropped her like a hot potato, I hear she had quite a following in the suburbs. She ended up doing well enough on her own."

"Except that she was strangled to death," Kate said. I almost smacked her.

The door chimes rang, and Margery looked to the front door as several women entered. "You will excuse me, won't you? We're a little short on staff."

When Margery walked out of earshot I elbowed Kate. "Do you think you could have brought up the murders many more times?"

"Not without looking suspicious," Kate said, lowering her voice, missing my point entirely. "Can you believe that Eleanor and Carolyn used to be business partners?"

"It does make the case more complicated."

Kate darted a look over her shoulder. "The pot thickens."

Chapter 15

"Parking is a nightmare." Richard breezed past the host stand at the Peacock Café and joined us at the window table we'd nabbed before the restaurant had gotten busy.

Kate and I had been watching the lights of rush hour traffic as we'd sipped our glasses of wine and waited for Richard to join us. Since the sun had set before most people got off work, it felt like nighttime instead of only happy hour. The bar sat behind an arched wood and glass partition to one side of the dining room and had filled up quickly with the stylish set.

"It's Georgetown," Kate said. "Parking is always a nightmare."

"Too true, darlings." Richard gave us each a pair of air kisses before sitting down. He'd recently taken up the European custom of kissing on both cheeks as a tribute to his French heritage. Not that any of his ancestors had set foot in France for the past few generations.

Richard ordered a Campari and soda from the closest passing waiter and relaxed into his low wooden chair.

"Stressful day?" I asked.

"You have no idea." Richard slipped his black jacket off and rolled up the sleeves of his melon green shirt. "Jim's flying squirrel got loose in the office."

"Was it Bring Your Illegal Pet to Work Day and no one told me?" Kate said.

Richard gave her a withering look. "Don't even ask why the creature was in the building to begin with because it will get me all whipped up."

I suppressed a smile. "Doesn't Jim keep him on a leash?"

Richard took his drink from the waiter before it reached the table. "Apparently, flying squirrels are nocturnal. He was supposed to sleep all day in the closet."

"The closet?" Kate asked.

Richard took a long drink. "In the pocket of Jim's coat, to be exact."

I pressed my lips together to keep from laughing. "That sounds like a foolproof plan."

"Doesn't it?" Richard raised an eyebrow.

"I hope for the squirrel's sake he didn't get loose in your office," I said. I could only imagine Richard's tolerance for a squirrel running amok in his pristine office, which consisted of a black wooden desk and two designer Plexiglas chairs.

Richard shook his head. "No, but suffice it to say that the animal had never seen a Christmas tree before."

"You didn't tell us you had your holiday decorations up already," Kate said. "What's your theme this year?"

Every year Richard decked his offices in his own totally unique spin on a theme that over the years had ranged from Bolshevik glamour to Tibetan chic.

"Christmas in the Casbah. It's an Arabic interpretation of the holidays."

Kate raised an eyebrow at me. "That should be interesting. I can't wait to see it."

"Well, don't bother." Richard drained his glass. "That insane squirrel ruined it all. He scattered the sand I'd put around the Christmas tree so it would look like it was sitting in the desert. My sand dunes are ruined. Then he ran up the tree and clung to the very top, bending it over until it almost touched the floor before he jumped off. Of course the tree snapped back and my camel tree topper flew across the room and crashed into the bay window. It was awful."

"You have a camel Christmas tree topper?" I bit the inside of my mouth to keep from laughing.

"It wasn't easy to find, believe me," Richard said. "Enough about my horrific day. You didn't stumble across any more corpses that you neglected to mention, did you?"

"Nope." I took a sip of my wine. "We had a normal afternoon for a change. After we met a bride for a final dress fitting, we bought a few last minute things for the wedding, and then came here."

Richard gave me a suspicious look. "I'm surprised you stayed away from trouble for an entire day."

"You should see some of the stuff they have at

the Wedding Shoppe," Kate said. "Did you know that you can get rhinestone-studded 'Bride' and 'Groom' thongs?"

Richard shuddered. "And people are afraid of gay marriage." He paused, and then narrowed his eyes at me. "Wait a second. What were you doing at the Wedding Shoppe?"

"We needed a guest book and ring bearer pillow and thought they'd have the best selection," I said.

"You've never shopped there before." Richard looked unconvinced. "Do you expect me to believe that you didn't go there to scout out information on Carolyn?"

"Wow. He's good," Kate said. "So much for pulling the wolf over his eyes."

"Wool, Kate." I rolled my eyes. "You pull the wool over someone's eyes."

"Really?" Kate said. "Well, that doesn't make any sense at all."

"I knew you couldn't resist the temptation to poke around in this murder investigation." Richard wagged a finger at me. "If you're not careful, you're going to be next."

"That's exactly why we're trying to find out who has it out for wedding planners and why," I said. "If there really is a serial killer on the loose, we're potential victims."

Richard tapped his chin. "You have a point. You have been a little too close to both murders for comfort."

"We're doing a little harmless information gathering," Kate explained. "We plan to tell anything we find out to the cops."

"Well?" Richard looked back and forth between us. "Did you find out anything good?"

Kate scooted to the edge of her chair. "Eleanor Applebaum used to be Carolyn's business partner and Carolyn got rid of her once the business started to take off."

"And?" Richard asked. "That's old news."

"Not to us," I said. "Why didn't you ever tell us?"

"Why bother? There's much better gossip than something boring that happened twenty years ago."

"Boring?" I asked. "I'll bet the police won't think the connection between the two murder victims is boring."

"They will once they find out *why* Eleanor left the business without much of a fuss," Richard said in a singsong voice. "That's not boring."

Kate leaned across the table. "You know?"

Richard nodded gleefully. "Rumor has it that Carolyn blackmailed her. Either Eleanor could leave quietly or Carolyn would make sure that everyone saw the pictures of her with Maxwell."

Kate's mouth dropped open. "Eleanor Applebaum and Maxwell Gray? The wedding photographer who always tries to seduce the bridesmaids?"

"And sometimes the bride," Richard muttered.

"He's very popular with wedding planners, too," I admitted. I'd heard rumors about my colleagues and the Don Juan of D.C.'s wedding world, although Eleanor really didn't seem like his type.

"Apparently he and Carolyn set her up," Richard continued. "The affair with Maxwell and the kinky photos were all part of Carolyn's plan."

"Why would Maxwell go to all that trouble to help Carolyn?" I asked. "I know she asked for commissions from vendors but that's a bit extreme."

"Probably because he and Carolyn had been having an on-again-off-again affair for years," Richard said. "There was a time he would have done anything for her. That was before her looks went, of course."

"I don't think I saw her before her looks went." Kate made a face. "Remind me to disinfect myself the next time I shake Maxwell's hand." Bold words coming from the woman who would have held the Guinness world's record for dating the most men consecutively, if there had been such a category.

"The two victims had a lot more in common than we first thought." I swallowed hard. "Finding what links them to the killer may not be such an easy feat after all."

Richard leaned over and patted our hands. "But your lives may depend upon it, darlings."

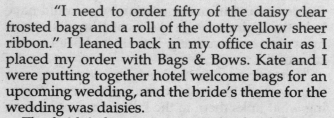

Chapter 16

"I need to order fifty of the daisy clear frosted bags and a roll of the dotty yellow sheer ribbon." I leaned back in my office chair as I placed my order with Bags & Bows. Kate and I were putting together hotel welcome bags for an upcoming wedding, and the bride's theme for the wedding was daisies.

The bride's bouquet was a clutch of daisies, sugar daisies would cover the wedding cake, and a pressed daisy adorned the top of her custom-made wedding invitations. It only made sense that the gift bags would feature daisies, but I felt very close to ODing on this wedding theme. In this case, Over Daisying.

The doorbell rang as I finished placing the order and hung up the phone. I glanced at the clock on my desk. Twelve-thirty. Too early for Kate to be back from the Container Store. I'd sent her off in the morning to buy bunches of little metal tins to hold the candies and snacks for the welcome bags.

Of course, it wasn't too early for me to have made it to the shower. I groaned as I looked down at the fleece pants and hoodie I'd thrown on that morning. I'd only intended to return a few phone calls before showering. That had been hours ago and I hadn't budged from my desk.

"Annabelle? Are you there?" I recognized the Scottish accent immediately. Ian.

I felt a wave of panic. I couldn't let him see me like this. "Hold on," I yelled. "I just got out of the shower."

I flew down the hall to the bathroom and turned on the shower full blast while I tore off my clothes. I jumped in before testing the water and almost screamed because it was so cold. I danced in and out of the water as I soaped up and rinsed off in record time. I pulled a smoke-blue towel off the rack behind the door and dried myself as I ran to my bedroom.

"I'm coming," I called out, throwing the towel to the floor and pawing through my underwear drawer. I clearly needed to do laundry because the only thing left in the drawer was the red mesh thong with white fringe that Kate had given me as a gag gift last Christmas.

"Great," I mumbled as I pulled it on. What kind of sadist designed thongs anyway? Especially ones with fringe.

I tugged on my Seven jeans and a long-sleeved black knit top. A thong and trendy jeans. Kate would be so proud. I ran back into the bathroom and swept on a coat of mascara, patted my face with pressed powder, and dabbed on some pink lip gloss. Tossing my head over, I fluffed my hair with my fingers then flipped it back up and let it fall into place. I looked in the mirror. Not bad for under five minutes.

"Coming," I said as I rushed down the hall and skidded to a stop in front of the door. I took a deep breath and opened it.

Ian leaned against the door frame in a pair of jeans and a tight black sweater that zipped in front. His blue eyes held mine as he smiled at me. I felt my knees wobble. Oh boy.

He stepped forward and wrapped one arm around my waist, pressing his body fully against mine. He brushed a strand of hair off my face and ran a finger down my cheek and neck, pausing at the hollow in my throat. My heart pounded so hard that I was sure he could feel it, and I had to remind myself to breathe.

"I've been thinking about you," he said, barely above a whisper.

I tried to say something but my mouth had gone dry.

"I left you a message earlier, but I decided that I had to come over and see you. I wanted to say hello and apologize in person for missing our date on Sunday."

If this was how he said hello, I was almost afraid of what would happen on an actual date. "You're forgiven," I managed to say.

"Is she okay?" Leatrice's voice jolted me from my trance. "Did she faint?"

Leatrice stood behind us in the hall wearing a

Santa sweatshirt and a green elf's cap with bells. I straightened up and took a step back. I had to remember to close the door in this building. Correction. Lock the door.

Ian's arm slipped from my waist and he turned to Leatrice. "She's fine."

Comprehension dawned on Leatrice's face, and she turned pink under her heavy rouge. "I'll leave you kids alone, then." She held out some folded-up pages of the newspaper. "I just came up to give Annabelle the newspaper clippings about the murders."

"Murders?" Ian turned to me, one eyebrow cocked. "That's what the police were doing at your apartment the other day?"

"I meant to tell you but it's been a little crazy," I said. "A wedding planner was killed at the Mayflower on Saturday and another at the OWP meeting on Monday...the Organization of Wedding Planners."

Ian's smile faded. "You were at both places?"

Leatrice nodded with enthusiasm. "She found both of the bodies. Isn't that exciting?"

"A coincidence," I said with a dismissive wave. "I barely even knew the first victim."

"Two wedding planners being killed in a few days time doesn't seem like a coincidence," he said.

"Who knew it was such a dangerous job?" Leatrice shook her head. "Annabelle's going to have to start packing heat in her emergency kit."

I tried not to laugh. Leatrice had been watching cop shows again.

Ian studied me for a second, then took my hand

in his and pressed it to his lips. "You'll be careful?"

"Of course." My voice came out as barely a squeak.

Ian gave me a slow wink. "Maybe you need a bodyguard."

"That's a great idea!" Leatrice bounced up and down on her toes, the bells of her elf cap jingling. "I could stay with you at night with my pepper spray and safety horn."

"No," I said a little too forcefully. "I'll be fine."

Ian leaned in close to me. "Maybe I should come over tonight and check on you just in case."

"Sure," I said. "Oh, wait. I forgot that I have to go to an industry party. I promised Richard I'd be there since he's catering."

"What about afterward?"

"Okay. I should be back by nine."

Ian stroked the top of my hand. "Until tonight, then." He kissed me lightly on the cheek, then left, closing the door behind him and leaving Leatrice inside.

She clapped her hands together. "This is so exciting, dear. It's been ages since you've had a date."

"How do you know?"

Leatrice raised an eyebrow at me. "I am the president of the neighborhood watch, remember?"

How could I forget? She asked visitors for their ID in the hall, and once she'd almost made a citizen's arrest when she thought a pizza boy looked suspicious.

"It's no big deal," I said.

"Are you kidding?" Leatrice began gathering the papers on my coffee table, making little jingling noises as she cleaned. "We need to do some serious work on this place before tonight. And you are planning on doing something with your hair, aren't you?"

"Of course. I've been working all morning and I just got out of the shower. I didn't have time to fix my hair yet." Why was I explaining this to Leatrice?

She gave me a relieved smile. "That's good to know, dear. Now where do you keep your cleaning supplies?" She paused and looked worried. "You do have cleaning supplies, don't you?"

Before I could protest, the phone in my office rang. I rushed down the hall and grabbed it before the call went to voice mail.

"Wedding Belles. This is Annabelle."

"Annabelle, it's Gail."

It took me a second to connect the voice to the OWP president. "Hi, Gail." I tried not to sound surprised that she'd called. Gail rarely made time for any of the new planners like me.

"Are you going to Maxwell's housewarming party for his new studio?"

"I planned to stop by," I said hesitantly. Since when did Gail care if I would be at an industry event?

"I heard you and Kate were trying to find out information about Carolyn." She lowered her voice. "I can't talk now but I have some information you might want."

People thought we were snooping around in

the murder investigation? That was the last thing we needed. "What kind of information?"

"Now isn't a good time. Someone could overhear me. Find me at the party."

Like that would be a good place for a quiet conversation. She probably wanted to tell me dirt I'd already heard. "I'm not really interested in more idle industry gossip, Gail."

"This isn't gossip. It's information that the police will want to hear and that Byron Wolfe would kill to keep quiet."

The phone went dead, and I dropped into my chair. Information that Byron would kill to keep from the police? Maybe he already had.

Chapter 17

"Gail really said that?" Kate asked as she maneuvered her car through the streets around U Street to find parking. Maxwell's new studio was in a loft near U Street, an area that had recently gone through a transformation from scary to stylish. "Why would she rat out her own partner?"

"They aren't really partners. They buddy up a lot."

"Still. I thought they were thick as leaves."

I raised an eyebrow. "Do you mean thick as thieves?"

"Whatever." Kate wedged her car into a marginally legal parking space. "Byron must have really done something to tick off Gail if she's willing to implicate him in the murders."

I stepped out of the car and readjusted my black wrap dress. "She didn't say that the information implicated him in the murders, only that he would kill to keep it quiet."

"Same thing." Kate clicked the alarm on her car and walked around to join me on the sidewalk. Her snug red angora sweater didn't leave anything to the imagination, but at least she'd paired it with simple black pants. Even if they were pretty form-fitting.

"It would be nice to find out something besides reasons why Carolyn and Eleanor would want to knock off each other," I said.

"No kidding. So far everything we've learned proves how much the two women hated each other." Kate led the way down the sidewalk, and I tried to keep up in my high heels. Now I remembered why I loved wearing flats, even though these shoes did make my legs look great. "Which would be helpful if they weren't both dead."

We reached a brick building with an arched entrance and Kate punched in a code on the entry keypad. The door buzzed and we went inside.

"Maxwell is at the top, right?" Kate looked around the small foyer for an elevator, and then her eyes settled on the staircase in front of us.

I sighed and slipped off my shoes. "The fifth floor."

We trudged up silently and paused to catch our breath when we reached the top.

"I really need to go to the gym," Kate panted.

"Do you belong to a gym?" I asked, slipping my shoes back on and pressing the doorbell.

"Fine. So I need to join a gym, too."

The door opened, and Jim smiled when he saw us. Richard's top banquet captain was tall and thin with a shaved head and pale blue eyes. I'd never seen him wearing anything but a tuxedo, and I had a hard time imagining him looking less than formal.

"Hey Jim, how's it going?" I stepped inside the studio.

Jim darted a glance over his shoulder. "Let me say that Richard will be glad to see you two."

"That doesn't sound encouraging," Kate said.

"I never knew that wedding planners could be so demanding." Jim shook his head. "Or drink so much."

"You'd be surprised." I took a look around the room.

With high ceilings, hardwood floors, and minimalist chrome and black furniture, the penthouse loft looked every bit the photographer's studio. It was a nice change from Maxwell's old office, which had been decorated to look like a harem. Of course, the harem look fit his personality better. I wondered how his seduction routine would work in such stark surroundings.

I gave the crowd a cursory glance and saw the usual suspects. It looked like an OWP meeting with dimmer lights and fancier clothes. I reminded myself that I definitely wanted to stay alert tonight because parties for people who planned parties usually got pretty wild. Maybe the fact that we could rarely attend a party and actually have a drink made wedding planners get a little out of control. Whatever the reason, I'd seen enough at past parties to know to keep my wits about me.

Richard saw us from across the room and

rushed over. "Remind me never to cater an industry party again. Party planners are the worst guests."

Kate suppressed a smile. "They're giving you trouble?"

"Some of the guests are complaining that there are too many carbs, while the vegetarians are upset that there's too much meat. They're impossible." Richard held up his hands. "And the worst part is they're all three sheets to the wind and starting to get way too friendly with each other."

Kate tugged at my sleeve. "Is that Alexandra dirty dancing in the corner with Maxwell's assistant?"

I cringed as I recognized our favorite cake baker getting very friendly with the handsome Latin photographer. They both looked pretty tipsy and were getting friendlier by the moment. I looked at my watch. "How late are we?"

"People arrived early and haven't given the bartenders a moment's rest," Richard said. "It isn't pretty. Frankly, I can't believe I wore Dolce & Gabana for this."

A waiter came up and whispered in Richard's ear. He gave an impatient sigh. "I don't know why I bother to write up event timelines if no one reads them. I'll be right back." He pointed a finger at me. "Don't even think of leaving."

Kate turned to me after Richard left. "Should we try to fight our way to the bar?"

"Yoo hoo!" Fern's voice carried above the crowd, and I recognized the enormous rings on his hand waving above people's heads. "Over here, girls."

We pushed our way to where Fern stood next

to a high-top table draped in silver lamé. He wore a green velvet suit with a tapered jacket and peg pants, and had an enormous opal pendant around his neck.

He pulled us close to him. "I would have come over to you but this crowd is getting a little rowdy, and some of the women have been giving me funny looks."

"How drunk are these people?" Kate said.

"Well, our host has been knocking back martinis since I arrived." Fern motioned to where Maxwell sat on a dark leather couch with a woman in a low-cut black dress draped over him. His long blond hair was feathered off his face and he wore his gray silk shirt open almost to his waist. He reminded me of a slightly geriatric Fabio. "He's been getting quite friendly with that woman on his lap."

"That's Stephanie Burke." I put my hand over my mouth. I hadn't recognized her right away with her hair pulled up. Her trademark was her wild mane of curly hair, and she didn't look like herself with a sleek bun. "She's one of the newest wedding planners in the city. I didn't even know that she knew Maxwell."

Kate smirked. "It looks like she does now."

I shook my head "Poor thing. She hasn't been in the business long enough to know about his reputation."

"We could warn her if you happen to have a crowbar to pry them apart," Kate said.

"At least she's in good company," I said. "Half of the planners in this room have fallen prey to his charms."

Kate made a face. "I know he was supposed to

be handsome when he was younger, but he must be at least fifty or sixty by now."

"I don't think he's gotten the memo," Fern said. He made a megaphone with his hands. "If your chest hair is gray, doll, it's time to button up the shirt."

I averted my eyes from Maxwell. "Is there anyone he hasn't made a move on?"

Kate nudged me. "Lucille and Margery."

"I wouldn't be so sure," I said. "He's an equal opportunity Casanova."

"No, I meant look, it's Lucille and Margery."

"You're kidding." I peered through the crowd to where the women sat at a cocktail table looking like the only other sober people at the party. "I didn't think Lucille could manage to look sadder, but she does."

"I don't blame her," Fern said. "She did just lose her job."

Kate and I turned to him. "What?"

"Didn't you hear? Carolyn's husband inherited the Wedding Shoppe and decided to sell the business. He gave everyone notice this morning. I guess the business won't close right away, but they have to find new jobs soon."

"That's horrible," I said. "Poor Lucille and Margery. They've worked there for almost twenty years."

"I didn't even know Carolyn was married," Kate said.

"I don't think she and her husband got along too well," Fern said. "She would be spinning in her grave if she knew he planned to sell the business she spent years building."

"I would have thought she'd leave it to Lucille and Margery." Kate glanced over at the two subdued women. "After all their hard work, it would have been the nice thing to do. Especially if she didn't get along with her husband."

"I doubt she thought she'd die so soon," I reminded her. "And Carolyn wasn't known for being fair or nice."

Fern's mouth twitched up in a smirk. "She probably planned to take everything with her. We always say that this is a job from hell."

"But why get rid of it so fast?" Kate shook her head. "I'm sure the store makes a decent profit."

"He must not have wanted to run a wedding planning company," I said. "Even a successful one."

Fern tucked an errant strand of dark hair back into his ponytail. "I wonder who the buyer is."

"Whoever it is, they snapped it up pretty fast." I tapped my chin. "I guess now we know who benefited most from Carolyn's death."

"Her husband or the person who bought the business?" Kate asked.

"Both, I guess," I said. "Are you thinking what I'm thinking?"

"We need to find out who was so eager to buy the Wedding Shoppe," Kate said.

Fern rubbed his hands together. "I think we have some new suspects."

Chapter 18

"I get why Carolyn's husband would want her out of the way, but why would he kill Eleanor, too?" Kate asked. "Did he even know her?"

"Good point." I frowned. "It's not like Carolyn brought him to industry parties. We never even knew he existed."

"I knew he existed," Fern said. "She used to bring him around years ago when she first started out. Way before your time, darlings."

"What was he like?" I asked, curious about who the queen bee of wedding planning would pick for a husband.

Fern made a face. "Not very memorable. I think he was an accountant or he worked for the government. Something with numbers and a desk. Once Carolyn started becoming more successful, we never saw him again."

"It probably made it easier to have her fling with Maxwell without a husband lurking around," Kate said.

I made a face. "Stop bringing that up. It gives me the creeps to think about Carolyn and Maxwell."

Kate laughed. "Don't forget Maxwell and Eleanor."

I gave Kate a dirty look. "That still doesn't explain why Carolyn's husband would want to kill Eleanor as well as his wife."

Fern polished his huge square-cut topaz ring with the French cuff of his shirt. "Maybe the deaths aren't related."

Kate and I both looked at Fern in disbelief.

"Okay, okay." He looked up from his ring. "I'll admit the chances are slim."

"Wait a second," I said. "Maybe Carolyn's husband did know Eleanor. She and Carolyn were business partners at one point, remember?"

Kate rapped her fingers on the table. "And his motive for killing Eleanor would be?"

I thought for a moment. "I have no idea."

"Back to square run," Kate said.

Fern looked confused.

"My life is constant torture," Richard moaned as he joined us.

"What now?" I asked.

"The waiters mixed up the serving pieces in the back. They're serving the wild mushroom soup sips in the glass shooters."

"The horror." Fern rolled his eyes as he patted Richard on the shoulder.

Richard glared at him, and Fern slowly removed his hand. "The lobster and sake shooters were supposed to go in glass and the soup sips in the white demitasse cups. The mushroom soup looks awful in glass. It's like Baby's First Summer in a cup."

Fern made a face. "So much for eating mushroom soup again."

Richard put his head in his hands. "I can't believe they sent me the third string waiters. I'd have better luck getting staff from an insane asylum."

"They would probably be more entertaining, too," Fern said. "Nothing like crazy people to liven up a party."

Richard peeked out from behind his fingers long enough to give Fern a withering look. "I'm ruined. Of all the parties to mess up, they had to do it at the one with all the party planners."

"I'm sure it was an honest mistake," Kate said.

"This is a conspiracy." He took his hands down and glared at a passing waiter. "I'll teach them to mess with me. I'll have them working on children's birthday parties for the rest of their lives." He waved a finger at the waiter. "You, my friend, will be leading pony rides for the rest of your catering career."

I put a hand on his arm. "Take it easy, Richard. No one is conspiring against you."

Fern patted Richard. "You'd better calm down before you pull something."

"The important thing is that you're not overreacting," Kate said.

Richard straightened his shoulders. "I never overreact. You know I hate dramatics."

"Ten bucks he makes another waiter cry," Kate whispered to Fern behind her hand.

"Cry and run out wailing or just cry?" Fern asked her.

Richard ignored them and took a deep breath. "The staff isn't my only problem. Who are the high maintenance girls who refuse to eat cute animals? They made a huge scene when we passed out duck quesadillas."

"What?" I asked.

Richard pointed to two twenty-something women sitting with Lucille and Margery. They both had blond hair that had been blown straight, and they looked bored with life. "Apparently they aren't strict vegetarians. They just don't eat any animal that used to frolic. Their words, not mine. Luckily, they don't consider crabs or shrimp cute so they wolfed down the crab wontons with blackberry sauce and the Hawaiian barbecue shrimp with papaya."

My stomach growled and I looked around for a waiter with a tray of hors d'oeuvres. "Where is the food anyway?"

"Are you sure they aren't brides?" Kate said. "That sounds like bridal dementia to me."

"Those are the former sales girls from the Wedding Shoppe," Fern said. "They came with Lucille and Margery."

"The ones that Carolyn fired last week?" I asked.

"I guess so," Fern shrugged. "Not a cheery bunch, are they?"

"I don't really blame them," Kate said. "They did lose their jobs right before the holidays."

"I'm sure they'll be able to find a job in no time after working for Carolyn," I said. "Maybe that's why they came to the party. To find a job with another party planner."

"Do you think they'd consider being waiters?" Richard asked.

"Annabelle. Kate." Gail Gordan appeared at my shoulder but didn't look directly at us when she spoke. She wore a black dress cut deep enough to show off a huge emerald pendant around her neck. "Can we talk?"

"Sure," I said. "What did you want to tell me about Byron?"

She gave a curt shake of her head. "Not here. Meet me in the kitchen in a few minutes."

"She's a little secretive, isn't she?" Kate watched her walk away. "The dirt on Byron had better be worth it."

"Gail is full of surprises." I watched her pause in front of Maxwell and lean in close to talk with him. "She seems to know our host pretty well."

Richard nudged us. "They used to be very friendly with each other, if you know what I mean."

I watched as Gail pulled back from Maxwell and stalked off. "Is there anyone here who hasn't been his victim?"

"Speaking of victims, what happened to Stephanie?" Kate looked around for the perky young planner.

"Maybe she wised up," I said, and then turned to Kate. "Let's go meet Gail and get this over with."

Fern grabbed us by the sleeves. "Promise you'll come right back and tell us every word."

"We promise," I said.

I led Kate through the crowd, trying to avoid making eye contact with people. No time for chitchat. Luckily, Alexandra was so involved with the handsome, dark-haired photographer that she didn't even notice us pass by. Most of the guests seemed pretty drunk and more than a few people were getting very friendly with each other. I knew this party would provide enough gossip for the wedding industry to thrive on for months.

I pushed through the metal swinging door that led to the kitchen. The countertops and appliances were gleaming stainless steel and the cabinets were dark wood with metal knobs. The decor was minimalist and sleek without a hint of color. You could hardly get a more masculine kitchen without putting a grill or wide screen TV in the center.

A few waiters scuttled around refilling white ceramic platters from the pair of tall metal warmers in the corner. I saw a black lacquered tray of shot glasses filled with a milky gray liquid and shuddered. Richard was right. Glass and mushroom soup did not mix.

"Where is she?" Kate walked over to a platter of mini duck quesadillas and popped one in her mouth.

I glanced at my watch. It was past eight-thirty. "I need to go in a few minutes. I have a date."

Kate dropped a quesadilla on the black tile floor. "You have a date after this?" She put her hands on her hips. "What I am I supposed to tell Richard? He's going to be hysterical."

Before Kate could interrogate me, the swinging door hit me on the back and sent me forward a few steps.

"Hi, Gail." Kate looked up from scraping the quesadilla off the floor.

Gail stepped in the kitchen. "Sorry about that." I rubbed my back where the door had smacked me. She didn't seem too broken up about it. "I have to talk fast. I just saw Byron arrive."

"What's so important that we have to meet in secret?" Kate dropped the quesadilla in the trash and took a golden puffed samosa off a nearby platter. "And I thought you and Byron were friends."

Gail's cheeks reddened. "We were, I mean, we are. But I can't keep his secrets anymore. The lies are eating me up inside."

"What lies?" This coming from the most cutthroat, back-stabbing planner around.

"I lied to you the other day when I said that Byron joined me at St. Matthew's. He never showed up. I waited for him to help me with the processional but finally had to do it on my own. When I asked him what happened later, he gave me a weak excuse about the bride asking him to clean up the suite for her."

Kate took another samosa. "I don't know Byron very well, but cleaning doesn't sound like something he would do."

"Exactly. He would never risk breaking a sweat," Gail said. "He would have called housekeeping before he lifted a finger to clean the room."

"But why lie? What reason did he have to stay behind?" I asked.

"I don't know what happened," Gail said. "But Byron had plenty of reason to want Carolyn dead."

"Because he used to work for her?" Kate asked.

Gail shook her head. "Because Carolyn and Eleanor fired him."

I looked at Kate. "Eleanor?"

Gail nodded. "Eleanor was also Byron's boss. He blamed both of them for not making him a partner in the company. If there's one thing Byron is good at, it's holding a grudge."

"I heard that you still hold a grudge against Carolyn, too," Kate said. "Surely holding a grudge doesn't make someone a murderer, does it?"

Gail's eyes flashed with anger, but she kept her voice steady. "Whoever told you that I held a grudge against Carolyn is trying to make me look bad. That was ancient history."

Kate raised an eyebrow. "But what happened to Byron almost twenty years ago wasn't?"

"You don't know him like I do," Gail snapped. "He may seem charming on the surface but you don't want to witness his temper."

"It seems like lots of people around here act nice on the surface but have nasty tempers," Kate said. "Maybe it's a character trait of wedding planners in general."

Gail reddened. "I don't care if you believe me or not."

"Why not tell the police?" I asked. "Why tell us instead?"

"The police won't take me seriously since I have a history with Carolyn. The police seem to listen to you, though."

I looked at my watch. Almost nine o'clock. "What do you mean?"

Gail lowered her voice. "Everyone knows that you're trying to help out the cops by getting information on the victims."

"That's not true," Kate said. "The cops didn't ask us to poke around. We're doing it on our own."

That sounded even worse. I shot Kate a look. "We're not investigating anything, Gail."

She didn't look convinced. I wondered how many other people thought the same thing. As much as I wanted to stay and see what else Gail knew, I had to make it back to Georgetown to meet Ian. "Thanks for telling us about Byron. I have to run, but I'll pass the information on to the police."

I waved at Kate, who tried to protest through a mouthful of samosa, and I pushed the swinging door open. The door bumped into someone on the other side.

"I'm so sorry," I said.

"Don't worry about it, Annabelle." Byron stood on the other side of the door smiling at me. His white teeth were blinding against his bottle tan. "No harm done, right?"

I swallowed hard. This was not good.

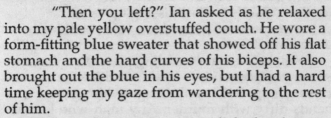

Chapter 19

"Then you left?" Ian asked as he relaxed into my pale yellow overstuffed couch. He wore a form-fitting blue sweater that showed off his flat stomach and the hard curves of his biceps. It also brought out the blue in his eyes, but I had a hard time keeping my gaze from wandering to the rest of him.

The butterflies in my stomach had only gotten worse since he'd arrived just minutes after I'd hopped out of the taxi and run up the three flights of stairs to my apartment. I'd barely had enough time to spray some lemon furniture polish in the air so the place would smell clean and throw some cheese and crackers on a tray before he'd rung the doorbell.

I set two glasses of the merlot he'd brought on my glass coffee table and took a seat next to him on the couch. "I probably should have warned Gail that Byron had been standing on the other side of the door, but it would have looked suspicious if I went back into the kitchen."

"Do you think he heard?"

"Maybe not," I said hopefully. "He'd just arrived at the party so he might have walked up to the door as I was leaving."

"He didn't say anything to you?"

I replayed my encounter with Byron in my head. "Not really, but the way he looked at me gave me the creeps."

Ian raised an eyebrow. "Was he hitting on you?"

"No. He only flirts with the party planners he thinks are the most important. That usually means the old guard. I haven't been around long enough for Byron Wolfe to start kissing up to me."

Ian's expression got serious. "Do you think he's dangerous?"

"Well, he's a male wedding planner, if that answers your question," I said. "I think he's a vicious gossip, but I can't imagine him getting his hands dirty with murder. Any man who knows as many different napkin folds as he does isn't the most testosterone-driven person around."

"You never know about people." Ian gave me a wicked grin. "They can surprise you."

I wasn't sure if he meant me or himself or was still talking about Byron. I barreled on. "I hope Gail and Kate aren't in danger."

"Do you believe what Gail told you about Byron?"

I thought for a second. "I'm not sure. She seemed genuinely nervous to be telling us, but she could be a good actress."

Ian took a sip of wine. "You said that she had a motive to kill Carolyn, too?"

"Pretty much the same as Byron. Carolyn fired her, but she claimed not to be upset about it anymore. The main difference between her and Byron is that he was fired by both victims, Carolyn and Eleanor."

"So he had motive for both murders?"

"Exactly," I said. "And according to Gail, he stayed behind at the hotel when Carolyn was killed, so he had opportunity."

"That does sound incriminating," Ian agreed. "He may be more capable of murder than he seems."

I chewed the edge of my lip. "I hope for Kate's sake that he's not."

"Your assistant stayed at the party?"

I nodded. "I tried to call her on her cell to tell her about Byron possibly overhearing us but she didn't pick up. It's probably so noisy she can't hear the ring."

Ian reached over and took my hand. "Don't give it a second thought, love. I'm sure you're worrying for nothing."

"You're right. The murders have made me a little high-strung."

Ian scooted closer to me. "Why don't I help you relieve some of that stress?"

My mouth fell open and I could swear that my heart actually stopped. I reached for my wine and took a gulp. I wasn't normally a big believer in self-medicating with alcohol, but in this case it seemed justified.

He took me by the shoulders and turned me around so I faced away from him. "Now close your eyes."

I gulped. Richard was right. He was into the kinky stuff. My hand began to shake so hard that I had to concentrate not to spill my wine all over the couch.

He started to rub my shoulders rhythmically, and I almost laughed with relief. He wanted to give me a back rub. Of course! I felt like kicking myself for thinking the worst.

"Is this better?" he said, leaning close to my ear.

I tried to speak but only managed a soft moan. I could feel the stress of multiple Bridezillas and monsters-in-law melting away as he massaged.

"I'm glad we finally have a chance to be alone." Ian pulled out my elastic hair band and my hair spilled down over my shoulders. "You've been on my mind since the moment we met, but I guess you hear that from a lot of guys."

"I'm a wedding planner," I managed to say. "The only men I meet are engaged or gay."

He laughed and ran both hands through my hair. "Well, I'm neither."

"Thank God," I muttered, my eyes still closed. Just as I felt myself completely melting, my cell phone began ringing.

"Ignore it," I said, not moving a muscle. It continued to ring, then stopped and started again.

"Someone really wants to find you," Ian said. "Are you sure you don't want to answer it?"

I sighed impatiently and reached for my purse on the floor. "If it's a bride, I'm going to put itching powder in her crinolines."

Ian took his hands out of my hair and leaned back against the couch. He grinned at me. "You do have a wicked side."

I found the phone and saw Richard's number on the caller ID. This had better be good. "Hi, Richard, what's up?"

"Annabelle, where are you?" He sounded hysterical, but what was new?

"Sorry I had to leave without saying good-bye, but I'm kind of busy right now. Can we talk tomorrow?"

"Don't hang up! I have to talk to you."

I cupped my hand over the mouthpiece. "I'm in the middle of something. Can't this wait?"

The doorbell rang and I groaned. Was this a joke?

I'll get it, Ian mouthed as he went to the door.

"If it's Leatrice, don't let her in," I whispered.

Ian smiled at me. "Don't worry."

"Okay, Richard." I turned from the door. "You have two seconds."

I heard the door open behind me and a voice that sounded much too deep to be Leatrice.

"Um, Annabelle," Ian said.

I spun around and saw Detectives Reese and Hobbes standing in the doorway, flashing their badges to Ian.

"That's what I've been trying to tell you, Annabelle," Richard said. "The killer struck again."

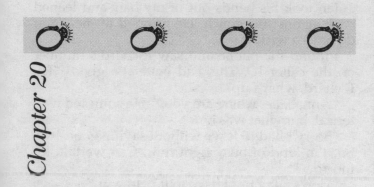

Chapter 20

"What do you mean there was a murder at Maxwell Gray's party?" The cell phone slipped from my hands and clattered to the floor. "I just came from there."

"We know." Detective Hobbes looked somber. "Do you mind if we ask you a few questions?"

Ian stepped aside to let the men in. Each wore blue jeans topped with a wool blazer, but Reese's black jacket looked stylish while Hobbes's brown tweed made him seem even more frumpy than usual. I motioned for them to take a seat while I scooped up the parts of my cell phone. I guessed I'd have to call Richard back later.

I sank onto the couch wordlessly while Detective Hobbes took out a pen and clicked it a few times. My head began to pound. I knew I should have warned Kate and Gail about Byron. He must have overheard us and decided to get rid of Gail before she could tell the police. If only I'd gone back and told them. But it was too late. I assured myself that Kate was fine. Byron didn't have as much of a reason to kill her, and he'd never try to get rid of them both.

Ian looked down at my shaking hands and took a seat next to me, draping an arm around my shoulders. Reese watched us then walked to the window while his partner took a seat across from me in the yellow armchair. Hobbes took a pocket-sized notebook out of his tweed blazer and clicked his pen a few more times.

I steadied my voice. "I don't know how much I can tell you, Detective. I wasn't even at the party when the murder took place."

"She's been here with me for the past half an hour," Ian confirmed.

Reese took in my mussed-up hair and high heels kicked off to the side of the couch. His eyes flitted to the glasses of wine on the coffee table. "I can see that."

My cheeks warmed and I shot Reese a defiant look, then turned away from him and focused on his partner. Why did I care what Reese thought of my personal life? Aside from a little harmless flirting and some definite chemistry, we'd never had any sort of relationship.

"Did you see Stephanie Burke while you were there?" Hobbes asked.

"Stephanie?" I looked back and forth between the detectives. "Why do you want to know about her?"

Hobbes looked up from his notebook. "Because she was found strangled with a camera cable in Mr. Gray's equipment closet."

My eyes widened. I could feel the blood rushing in my ears, and I breathed deeply to keep from getting sick. "Stephanie was murdered tonight?" I couldn't believe it. I'd been sure that the victim was Gail. Stephanie didn't make any sense. Who would want to kill her? I didn't think she'd been around long enough to make any enemies.

"Miss Archer?" Detective Hobbes waved a hand in front of me, and I heard his voice faintly through the ringing in my ears. "Did you see the deceased at the party tonight?"

I snapped back to reality. "Sure, I saw her. She hung out with Maxwell on the couch most of the time."

Hobbes scratched away in his notepad. "So they knew each other well?"

"I didn't think so, but they seemed very friendly tonight."

Reese walked over from the window. "Meaning?"

"Maxwell has a bit of a reputation," I explained. "He has a habit of becoming intimately involved with the party planners he works with."

"Interesting," Reese said.

"Not me, though," I added quickly. Ian reached over and squeezed my hand. "Mostly the older generation. That's why it's so odd that Stephanie got cozy with him tonight. I didn't even know she worked with him."

Hobbes flipped a page and continued writing. "Do you think some of the other planners might have gotten jealous?"

"I guess," I said. "I did see Gail have an argument with Maxwell tonight. Apparently they used to be an item. But I can't imagine someone killing over Maxwell."

Reese took a seat on the blue ottoman across from the couch. "Can you think of any other reason why someone would want to kill Miss Burke?"

I shook my head. "I didn't know her very well, but I can't see any connection between her and the other two murders. You do think this murder was committed by the same person, don't you?"

Reese locked onto me with his hazel eyes, and they deepened into green. "The M.O. is exactly the same. So unless we have a copycat killer, I'm assuming that the same person killed all three wedding planners."

"Do you have any leads?" Ian asked, and received a curt shake of the head from Reese.

I rubbed my temples. "It doesn't make sense. At least Carolyn and Eleanor had some connections to each other and some common enemies. Stephanie is completely out of left field."

"You can't think of anything the three women had in common?" Hobbes asked.

"Aside from a tenuous romantic link to Maxwell?" I thought for a moment. "Other than that, Stephanie doesn't fit with the other two at all. She was brand new to the wedding planning business and was very young and friendly. Not to mention pretty. She couldn't have been more opposite from Carolyn and Eleanor."

Hobbes looked up from his notes. "Sounds like you weren't big fans of theirs."

"I don't know that many people really liked Carolyn or Eleanor." I hoped I didn't sound defensive. "Most people were afraid of Carolyn and annoyed by Eleanor. But everyone liked Stephanie."

"This makes the situation even more dangerous." Reese rested his elbows on his knees.

"What do you mean?" I asked.

"Is Annabelle in danger?" Ian asked, and closed his fingers around my hand.

Reese kept his eyes on me. "The killer had established a type of victim with Carolyn and Eleanor. They had obvious connections, which meant that they also had similar connections to the killer. By killing Stephanie the killer seems to have abandoned the pattern."

"What if he killed Stephanie to throw you off the trail?" I asked.

Reese looked skeptical. "It's possible, but it's a big risk to take to confuse us."

I had to agree. Whoever had killed Stephanie in the middle of a crowded party had taken a huge chance of being caught. "So either Stephanie was killed to make it harder to find the killer or the murderer doesn't really have any pattern after all?"

Reese looked grim. "Either way, it isn't good."

"So any wedding planner could be killed next? Even if we have no connection to the other victims or the killer." I trembled and felt Ian's arm tighten around my shoulders. "This means that Kate or I could be next, doesn't it?"

Reese dropped his eyes to his hands and didn't answer. I glanced over at Hobbes, who didn't look up from his notebook. I had a sinking feeling in my stomach. Suddenly wedding planning wasn't such a dream job after all.

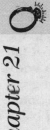

Chapter 21

"Are you sure you're okay to be here?" I asked Kate the next day as we walked down New York Avenue to the National Museum of Women in the Arts. "I can do the walk-through for Debbie's wedding without you."

Kate pulled her black fitted coat closed as the wind whipped around us. "Are you kidding? It's after noon so I'm sure Debbie and her mother have had their liquid lunch already. You're going to need all the help you can get."

"Richard will be here to keep things on track," I said.

"Like I said, you're going to need all the help you can get. I told you that I'm fine. I didn't even see Stephanie's body. Once the police asked me a few questions, I ran out of there."

"Okay, but don't forget that we're going to stop by Carolyn's viewing right after this."

Kate made a face. "Now that you mention it, I do feel a bit of a headache coming on."

I shook a finger at her. "You lost your window of opportunity."

Kate mumbled something that sounded a lot like "tyrant" as we reached the glass doors to the museum and ducked inside. Kate let her coat fall open to reveal knee-high black boots and a body hugging pink sweater dress. I avoided baring my legs when the weather was so cold and had opted instead for black wool pants and a cropped black and white tweed jacket

I did feel like a nun next to Kate's sexy outfit, though. I felt that way a lot next to Kate.

"Thank you very much for returning my calls last night." Richard came up to us in the museum's marble foyer but refused to meet my eye.

I smacked myself on the forehead. I knew there was something I'd forgotten to do. "I'm sorry, Richard. The police were at my apartment for a while and then I had to say good-night to Ian. I was so tired when everyone left that I collapsed."

Richard pulled himself up to his full height. "Excuse me. Did you say Ian? Were you on a date with him despite my warnings?"

"This should be good," Kate said.

"He may have a few tattoos and be in a band, but he's a nice guy," I said.

"Do you mean to tell me that I'm being replaced by a Johnny-come-lately who doesn't even know the difference between Prada and Pucci?"

I sighed. "You're not being replaced."

"I beg to differ." He waved a finger in the air. "You've never forgotten to return my calls before."

"I said I was sorry, Richard. It was an honest mistake."

Richard held up a hand. "He's already coming between us. I can see that now. You're going to kick all your faithful friends to the curb. Is that the way it's going to be, Annabelle?"

"Out with the old, in with the blue," Kate said.

Richard shook his head and I frowned at her. "It was only one date and it didn't even go very well."

"Why not?" Kate asked. "Did you take my advice about the cookie dough?"

Richard looked scandalized. "I don't even want to know what the cookie dough is for, but I hope you're not taking dating advice from Kate."

Kate stuck her tongue out at Richard. "For your information, Mr. Too Tight Pants, the cookie dough is to put in the oven so her apartment will smell good. It makes men think you're more domestic."

Richard looked down at his tapered blue pants and sucked in his breath. "I'll have you know that skinny pants are in."

Kate turned back to me. "So what went wrong?"

"Well, any date that ends with the police showing up at your door isn't a success in my book."

"Really?" Kate winked at me. "You should borrow my book for a while. The rules are a bit more relaxed."

Richard stifled a laugh. "A bit?"

Kate glared at him, and then turned back to me. "So nothing happened at all?"

"Well, not exactly nothing," I admitted. "Things

were moving in the right direction until Detectives Reese and Hobbes showed up."

"Spare me the details," Richard said. "We're here to work, you know."

The glass doors behind us opened, and two huge men dressed entirely in black leather strode through them. They wore riding goggles pushed up on their heads and looked identical from a distance except for the color of their goatees. One was red and the other dark brown.

"At least the florists are here," Richard said.

"Are we late, girls?" Mack rushed up, his face flushed almost as red as his hair. "Parking was impossible."

"Even for the Mighty Morphin Flower Arrangers," Buster said, referring to their unofficial name. They usually had an easier time with parking since they drove motorcycles.

The actual name of their company was "Lush," and they turned out some of the city's most cutting-edge floral designs. They were the first florists I knew who'd refused to put flowers in baskets and the only florists I knew who rode matching black and chrome Harleys.

I looked at my watch. "You're fine. Debbie and Darla are running a little behind."

"You didn't try to call us, did you?" Mack asked. "We got new cell phones so the numbers you have won't work anymore."

"Why?" Kate said. "You know you can keep your old numbers when you get a new phone."

Buster shook his head. "We changed the numbers on purpose to escape from an M.O.B."

Richard's eyebrows shot up. "You changed

your cell phone numbers because of a Mother of the Bride?"

Mack folded his arms across his massive chest. "Don't give me that look. You have no idea what this woman was like. She called so often that we couldn't get any work done."

"If I hadn't gotten a call in over an hour, I assumed my phone was broken," Buster added. "She made our lives hell."

"Don't curse," Mack scolded. Their Christian biker gang frowned upon cursing, and they were pious to the point that they considered "hell" a curse. Luckily they didn't have a hard and fast rule against badmouthing clients.

"You don't have to explain to me," I said. "I've had my share of awful M.O.B.'s."

Mack put a hand on my arm. "But we love this one. Drunks are so much fun."

"I wish all our clients drank as much as they do." Kate gave Mack a nudge and the two began giggling.

"Hush." Buster looked over his shoulder.

"I don't think it's a huge secret, boys," I said. "The entire theme for this wedding is booze. We have mint juleps before the ceremony, a bourbon tasting bar during cocktails, and a rum-soaked groom's cake and chocolate martinis passed for dessert."

"I hope no one lights a cigarette," Kate said. "The whole place will go up in flames."

"We're here!" Darla's voice carried from the entrance as she attempted to hold the glass doors open for her daughter. They both looked a bit unsteady.

Richard rushed forward. "Allow me." He held open the doors as the women teetered past.

"Aren't you precious?" Darla blew a kiss behind her.

"Did we miss anything?" Debbie clutched her Burberry bag in front of her and swayed slightly. Her mother had an identical handbag, and I noticed that the women wore matching Burberry headbands in their dark brown hair. "Lunch at Vidalia ran a teensy bit long."

My stomach growled at the mention of the Southern-inspired restaurant. It was a shame that the ladies had probably never sampled the world-class lemon chess pie. I doubted they'd actually ingested anything at the restaurant that didn't come in a martini glass.

Darla leaned on Buster's arm. "We had a floral inspiration while we were sitting at the bar."

Leave it to Darla and Debbie to get inspiration on a bar stool.

Debbie clapped her hands. "We want to recreate the wall of magnolias that they have behind the bar."

Mack looked around at the towering marble hall of the museum flanked by two sweeping stairways. "Where do you envision putting up a magnolia wall?"

Darla waved toward the opposite end of the hall. "We thought it could go behind the band as a backdrop."

Mack fiddled with his goatee. "That could work." He walked forward a few steps, and we all followed him into the main hall. "I see a matching garland of magnolia draping across the front and coming down the banisters."

"Perfect," Debbie said. "Now where are we putting the bars?"

Richard stepped forward with the floor plan. "Since you wanted more bars than we normally would do for two hundred guests, we have two down here with the bourbon bar and two upstairs."

"Shouldn't we have a bourbon bar upstairs as well?" Darla asked, digging in her purse. She produced a miniature cocktail shaker covered in pink crocodile. "I'd hate for guests to have to hunt around for it."

Richard made a few marks on the floor plan. "So that makes two bourbon bars, one up and one down."

I tried not to gawk as Darla shook the cocktail shaker vigorously. Was she going to make herself a drink in the middle of the museum?

"Perfect," Debbie said. "Now let's talk about the decorative ponies."

All of our mouths dropped open as we stared at the women. Darla took a swig from her shaker.

"I'm sorry." Buster gave his head a jiggle as if to clear his ears. "Did you say ponies?"

"That's right." Debbie hopped up and down. "We thought another way to personalize the wedding would be to have miniature ponies wandering around the cocktail hour for guests to pet. I used to love horses as a girl. You did say that we should bring personal elements into the wedding, didn't you, Annabelle?"

Richard gave me a sugary sweet smile. "Well, Annabelle?" He was loving this.

Mack turned to me. "Technically, ponies wouldn't fall under decor."

Oh no. He wasn't pawning this off on me. Where would I find midget horses?

"I think they would since they're called 'decorative ponies,'" I said.

"They're not decorative unless they have flowers on them," Mack countered.

"What a wonderful idea!" Darla said. "We should have floral wreaths around the ponies' necks."

Kate grinned at Buster and Mack. "Ponies as floral decor. What will you think of next?"

"You don't want to know," Buster grumbled.

"As great an idea as this is, I doubt the museum will go for it." I watched the women's faces fall.

"Decorative ponies would also require special permits," Richard said. "Now if you wanted to use dogs or cats, that's another matter, but horses, sheep, and ducks need a permit."

Not surprising that Richard would know this. He had a knack for knowing every obscure city rule and ordinance, which came in handy when clients made odd requests.

I jumped in before Debbie got the urge to have cats wandering around her wedding. I could imagine sounds of hissing and yowling cats wafting above the string quartet. Not to mention the number of extra Band-Aids I'd need for all the guests who'd get scratched. "I think you have plenty of personal touches already. Not every wedding has a cake in the shape of the groom's dog."

Debbie didn't look convinced. "Well, if you're sure we don't need the ponies …"

"Oh, I'm sure." I gave them a reassuring smile. "Trust me."

"Of course we do, darling. If it doesn't work, it doesn't work." Darla took a final drink from her cocktail shaker and dropped it back in her Burberry bag. Now I knew why she always carried an oversized purse. "Can you finish up the rest without us? We have tennis in half an hour."

"We're as good as done," I said, and followed the women back to the front doors.

"I'll send you the revised floor plan this afternoon," Richard said.

Buster adjusted the goggles on his head. "And we'll add the magnolia wall and garland into the proposal and send you a new copy."

"Don't forget the ponies," Kate said under her breath, and got glares from both Buster and Mack.

"No rush, dolls." Darla gave both men a smile that looked a bit like a leer.

"Fabulous to see you all." Debbie blew air kisses as she followed her mother's weaving path out of the museum.

Once the doors had closed behind the women, Kate let out a long breath. "Wow. They're really off their knockers."

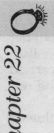

Chapter 22

"I'm not feeling so great after all." Kate slumped down in the passenger seat of my car and pressed her hand to her forehead. "Maybe I should skip Carolyn's viewing."

Richard reached from the backseat and felt her head. "You're fine. If I have to go, you have to go." He turned to me. "Why do we have to go again?"

"Because it's the right thing to do and it will be the perfect chance to find out more information about Carolyn." I pulled out of the parking garage and merged into traffic on Twelfth Street. "I'm sure all the suspects will be there since her memorial service is on Saturday and we all work."

Kate moaned and pressed her head against the window.

"Nice try, Kate," I said. "You're coming."

"What happened to the outpouring of sympathy I got this morning?" she said. "I was involved in a murder last night, remember?"

"Oh, please." Richard hated when anyone else got overly dramatic. "Being within the general vicinity of a corpse does not make you involved. I'm the one whose party was ruined."

"That's right," I said as I cut over onto Massachusetts Avenue. "You're taking this pretty well considering someone died at your event."

Richard shrugged. "She was strangled. No one can blame the caterer for that."

"Poor Stephanie," I said. "I still can't believe she's dead. Why would anyone want to kill her?"

"Well, she never sent me any business," Richard said. "I'm not asking for every party, but she could have thrown me a bone."

"How much business could she have had?" I said. "She was really new to weddings."

"Didn't she have a business partner when she started?" Kate asked.

Richard snickered. "You mean last month?"

I looked at him in the rearview mirror. "That's not nice. We haven't been around long, either. I think the other girl must have been her assistant because she looked even younger than Stephanie."

"Talk about the blind needing the blind," Kate said.

"I think that's 'leading the blind.'" Richard stuck his head between the two front seats. "Add one more person and they could call it the Three Blind Mice Agency."

I scowled at both of them as they collapsed into laughter. "You're awful."

Kate regained her composure. "Maybe the other planners were jealous because Stephanie was so young and bouncy."

"Do you really think someone strangled her because she was perky?" I gave Kate a sideways glance. We went around Dupont Circle and continued down Massachusetts. "That doesn't seem like much of a motive."

Kate turned the heat up in the car. "Have you considered that maybe these are all random, unconnected deaths?"

"They can't be unconnected." Richard leaned forward and stuck his head between our seats again. "All the victims are wedding planners. Maybe some deranged bride whose wedding was ruined by her wedding planner is on a rampage."

I glared at him in the rearview mirror as he sat back in his seat. "Thanks, Richard. That's comforting."

He gave me a smug grin. "Just trying to do my part to solve the crimes."

"Let's think this thing through," I said. "We know that Carolyn and Eleanor had some things in common and some mutual enemies."

"They both started the Wedding Shoppe and Byron worked for them before he got fired." Kate started counting on her fingers.

"Don't forget that Gail worked at the Wedding Shoppe, too," Richard said.

Kate whistled. "Did anyone in the wedding business not work for the Wedding Shoppe?"

"I forgot about Gail," I said as we drove down Embassy Row. "Did she work there with Eleanor or did she come afterward?"

Richard tapped his chin. "Afterward, I think."

"Remember that Margery said that she and Lu-

cille had just started working at the store when
Carolyn got rid of Eleanor," Kate said. "She didn't
mention Gail being there at the same time."

"So we have Byron, Gail, and Eleanor all getting
fired by Carolyn." I said. We turned onto Wisconsin Avenue and passed the National Cathedral.
"Any one of them could have killed her."

"Except Eleanor was murdered, so she can't be
the killer," Kate reminded me.

"You're forgetting Lucille and Margery," Richard said.

Kate turned around in her seat. "Are you kidding? Why would they kill Carolyn? They seemed
to worship her, and now that she's gone, they're
going to lose their jobs."

"If you ask me, anyone who worked for Carolyn
would have a reason to kill her," Richard said.

"I don't see their motivation," I said. "They had
the most to lose with Carolyn dead."

"What about those two sales clerks that Carolyn fired the week before she died?" Kate asked.
"We should put them on the list of suspects."

I raised an eyebrow. "I think it's a stretch, but
I guess we should include them. And there's Carolyn's husband, who inherited everything she
owned. Money is a pretty strong motive."

"And the mystery person who bought the Wedding Shoppe." Kate wagged a finger at me. "You
know what they say. Leave no stone unburned."

Richard rolled his eyes. "Oy." I could tell when
he'd been catering bar mitzvahs.

I stopped at a red light and leaned against the
steering wheel. "I'd love to find out who snapped
up Carolyn's business. Maybe the murderer plot-

ted against Carolyn because they wanted the business, not because they hated her."

"And they killed Eleanor and Stephanie because they'd gotten the hang of it?" Kate asked.

"My theory has a few holes," I admitted. "So we have a slew of people who could have killed Carolyn, but only Byron had it out for both Carolyn and Eleanor. And none of them had a reason to kill all three wedding planners. Either we're overlooking something that connects them to each other or the killer is someone we haven't even thought of yet."

Richard sighed. "You're completely forgetting that Maxwell had a link to all the women."

"If Maxwell killed everyone he'd seduced, half the population of the city would disappear," Kate said.

"Maybe he didn't kill them, but the killer had some reason to kill women that Maxwell has been involved with." Richard rolled down his window. "It's stifling in here."

"Do you mean like a psychotic former lover who decides to kill every other woman who has been in his life?" Kate wrapped her coat around her. "Now it's freezing."

"Not all of us are wearing micro minis," Richard complained as he rolled his window back up.

"That would almost be a relief because then we would be in the clear," I said. Kate remained silent. "Wouldn't we?"

"Of course," Kate gasped. "I do have my standards, you know."

Richard opened his mouth to say something,

and Kate whirled around and pointed a finger at him. "Not a word."

He held up his hands and assumed his most angelic face. "I wouldn't dream of it, darling."

"Carolyn's viewing is going to be the perfect place for us to find out who had the strongest motives," I said. "All the suspects will be there, I'm sure."

"You want us to question people who are there to mourn?" Kate asked.

"This is Carolyn," Richard reminded us. "I doubt too many people will actually be mourning."

"This may be the only time we'll have everyone in one place, including Carolyn's husband," I said. "It will be the perfect time to see who's acting suspicious or guilty. Then we narrow down the suspects and the motives and we'll have found our killer."

Richard didn't look so sure. "Let's hope the killer doesn't find out what we're up to first."

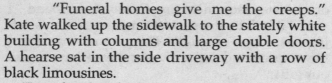

Chapter 23

"Funeral homes give me the creeps." Kate walked up the sidewalk to the stately white building with columns and large double doors. A hearse sat in the side driveway with a row of black limousines.

"I prefer the old-fashioned term 'funeral parlor,'" Richard said. "Makes it sound more festive."

"Cut it out, you two." I stopped outside the front doors and gave them each a warning look. "We're here to find out as much as we can about the victims and what they might have in common. It could be our only chance to have all the suspects in one place."

"Can I go on record for saying that stirring up information about a murderer is not a great idea?" Richard said. "You might make yourselves the next targets."

"We're going to be subtle, not broadcast to the world that we're searching for clues," I said. "Anyway, if we don't find out who's killing wedding planners, we could be next whether we investigate or not."

Richard put his hands on his hips. "You don't think our detective friends can find the murderer without your help, or would it be too much to ask you not to nose around in a mystery?"

"There is a difference between being nosy and gathering information," I protested. "The police can't move in the same industry circles that we can, otherwise I'd let them have at it. Anyway, no harm ever came from asking a few questions."

"Where have I heard that before?" Richard muttered.

"There you are." Fern rushed out the front doors waving his monogrammed handkerchief. That thing had really been getting a workout lately. "I've been waiting for you."

I looked at my watch. "Are we late? We had to do a walk-through."

Fern gave us all weepy hugs. "It's awful in there."

Kate gulped. "Lots of crying?"

"No." Fern lowered his voice. "They put Carolyn in a shiny white casket with gold trim. It looks like she's in a Camry."

Richard's mouth gaped open and he pushed past us to go inside. "This I have to see."

We followed Richard into the foyer of the funeral home and were greeted solemnly by an employee in a dark suit with a white carnation boutonnière. The building was carpeted in wall-to-wall light blue plush that muffled our footsteps and gave me the urge to whisper. Several groupings of conservative navy blue and beige living room furniture were placed throughout the spacious lobby, and marble busts sat on small platforms jutting out from the walls.

"Carnations," Kate whispered to me.

Fern let out a low whistle. "Don't be alarmed, girls. They're everywhere."

Carolyn would have died at the thought of a supermarket flower being at her funeral. All we had to do was add some baby's breath and the horror would be complete.

"Crabbe is this way." Richard pointed to the sign directing guests to various rooms and he led the way down the hall and past several closed sets of double doors. A pair of columns with marble busts stood at waist level outside each viewing room. This place was really big on the Classical era. I wondered if there were bodies in all of these rooms. As we got to the end of the hall, I could hear the buzz of voices getting louder.

Fern grabbed us by the arms before we reached the wide doorway to the viewing room with two marble heads on either side. "I have to warn you about Carolyn."

"You don't have to worry about me going anywhere near the body," Kate said.

Fern turned to me. "I don't want you to be surprised. It's pretty crowded in the casket. They're burying her with her day planner, cell phone, and wedding day walkie-talkie."

"Excuse me?"

Fern elbowed me. "I guess she planned to coordinate weddings from the beyond."

"Talk about being a workaholic," Kate said.

"When they say you can't take it with you, I

guess they don't mean work," Richard said. I could see that they were both trying hard not to laugh.

I elbowed them. "Get it together, you two. We can't go in there giggling."

"You won't be laughing once you see the Camry." Fern went into the room and motioned for us to follow.

He had vanished into the sea of people by the time Kate and Richard had stopped giggling and we'd stepped into the viewing room. I could see the bright white and gold casket gleaming against the far wall surrounded by sprays of flowers and wreaths on stands. I recognized some of the wedding industry regulars like Maxwell holding court with his usual gaggle of young women, but also a lot of unfamiliar faces. They must have been friends and family, but I had a hard time imagining Carolyn having a life outside of wedding planning.

"Why don't we split up?" I said to Kate and Richard. "That way we can talk to more people."

"I'm going to get a better look at that casket." Richard set off across the room before I could stop him.

"I'll go talk to Byron." Kate tugged the neckline of her sweater dress down. "He may be known for flirting, but two can play at that game."

Byron Wolfe might have been the biggest kiss-up in the business, but no one could flirt more shamelessly than Kate. If anyone could charm information out of him, she could.

I took a moment to scan the crowd. Gail and Botox Barbie seemed deep in conversation and kept glancing over at Byron. Gail seemed more than a little jittery, and Barbie seemed more than a little drunk. Did the funeral home have a bar?

"Good turnout, huh?"

I jumped at the sound of the voice behind me. I turned to find my videographer friend Joni with a camera in her hand. She wore black from head to toe, which was her usual work uniform at events and happened to be good funeral attire.

"You're videotaping the viewing?" I asked.

"Oh, sure." She nodded and brushed her sandy blond hair off her face. "People have me video all sorts of things. Usually they want to remember the eulogies but I've had requests to tape viewings before."

I shuddered. "Do you film the casket?"

"No way. I draw the line at dead bodies."

I lowered my voice. "So which is better? Working a wedding or a funeral?"

"No question. A funeral. Dead people are much less demanding than brides."

"Maybe I'm in the wrong business. Is there such a thing as a funeral planner?"

Joni laughed. "I'd better get back to work." She lifted her camera. "Carolyn's husband is looking over here. But find me later. I've got some great dirt for you."

I looked around for someone who could be Carolyn's husband. "Which one is he?" I asked, but Joni had already moved out of earshot. I reminded myself to touch base with her later. She always had the best industry gossip.

I scanned the crowd for anyone else I might

know. The two high-maintenance sales girls that
Carolyn had fired stood off in one corner whisper-
ing and flipping their blond hair. I wondered why
they'd bothered to show up if they despised their
former boss so much. Unless they were cruising
for a new employer among the crème de la crème
of Washington's wedding industry. I hoped they
didn't approach Richard. He was still fuming over
their protest on behalf of cute animals.

Lucille stood by herself a few feet away and
gave me a tiny wave, then blew her nose into a
tissue. I couldn't imagine Lucille having the nerve
to kill anyone, but it couldn't hurt to talk to her,
considering the fact that she'd worked with two
of the victims. I walked over and gave her a hug.

"It's so good of you to come." She dabbed at
her puffy eyes. "You and Kate have been so good
to us since Carolyn's death."

"It's the least we can do. Is Margery here, too?"
Usually the women were inseparable.

Lucille bobbed her head up and down and blew
her nose again. "She's mingling." She dropped her
eyes to the floor. "I think she's asking the other
planners if they have any openings. Would you
happen to need two experienced assistants?"

My heart went out to her. How awful to be
hunting for a job at the point in your life when
you should be thinking about retiring on a
sunny island. "We're a pretty small company," I
explained. "Wedding Belles is a two person op-
eration."

"I understand," Lucille said quickly. "Margery told me to save my money like she did, but

I wasn't able to give her as much to invest as I should have. I love to spoil my grandchildren. You know I have twelve."

I had no idea, and I felt a twinge of guilt that I knew so little about my colleagues. I touched her arm. "If we decide to expand, you'll be the first people we call."

Tears began to course down Lucille's cheeks. "I'm sorry to be such a wreck. It's been a lot to take in. First Carolyn, then Eleanor and that poor little Stephanie. Plus, after almost twenty years of service, Mr. Crabbe decides to sell the business and gives us notice that we need to find new jobs."

I put an arm around her shoulder. I really couldn't imagine what a horrible week she'd had. "Is Carolyn's husband here?"

Lucille nodded through her tears and pointed at a short, balding man next to the door.

I squinted at him and the woman in a brown jacket next to him. "The one talking with Margery?"

"I hope she's giving him a piece of her mind." Lucille sniffled and wiped her nose with a ragged tissue. "We should have gotten a paycheck this week and he hasn't paid us yet. He's so stingy that I wouldn't be surprised if he tries to get away with not paying us at all."

"Why don't I get you some more tissues?"

Lucille looked absently at the soggy one in her hands. "That would be nice, dear."

As I left Lucille, I noticed that Kate had cornered Byron and seemed to be either interrogating him or setting a date. Richard was nowhere to be seen, and I hoped he was talking to people and not just gawking at the gaudy casket. I feared that the combination of white and gold might send him over the edge.

As I passed Margery and Mr. Crabbe, it sounded like Margery was giving him more than just a piece of her mind, but Carolyn's husband seemed unmoved by her hissed threats about lawyers and payments. I headed back out to the hall to get Lucille some tissues since I remembered seeing a sign for a ladies' room when we'd come in. I passed a couple of closed doors, then one that stood ajar.

I was curious to see inside the other rooms. Did they have caskets in them already? I pushed the door open and poked my head in the dark room. The light from the hallway spilled in, but I still couldn't make out much. I stepped inside and felt along the wall for a light switch, and the door swung shut, leaving me in darkness. Great. Maybe this wasn't such a good idea after all. Richard would never let me hear the end of it if I got trapped inside a viewing room with a dead body.

I felt my way back to the entrance and had just reached it when the door opened and light poured into the room, blinding me for a second. I blinked a few times and saw a silhouette looming in the doorway before feeling a thud. I instinctively raised my hand to the side of my head, and everything went black.

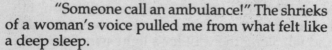

Chapter 24

"Someone call an ambulance!" The shrieks of a woman's voice pulled me from what felt like a deep sleep.

I tried to open my eyes, but the bright lights made my head pound even worse. I moaned.

"One of them is alive. Hurry!"

Was she talking about me? Wait a second. *Them?* I forced my eyes open and found myself staring at a white stucco ceiling. I rolled my head to one side and saw a mahogany casket at the far end of the room. It must have been the viewing room I'd been poking around in right before someone knocked me out. I rubbed my temple and rolled to the other side. My blood went cold.

Only a few inches away from me lay Margery with a red gash across her forehead. Her eyes were closed and her head lolled to the side. I felt like I was going to be sick. I closed my eyes and took a deep breath. I could hear people starting to gather around me.

"Coming through, people." Fern's voice was unmistakable. "I'm a hairdresser. I'm used to trauma."

I opened my eyes and pushed myself onto my elbows as Fern kneeled down next to me. "How bad is it?" I touched the tender spot on my head.

"I'm not going to lie to you, darling." Fern inspected my bump. "It's not pretty. The good news is that you've had worse hair days."

"Thanks." I sat all the way up and leaned against him. People began to cluster around Margery, who didn't seem to be moving. "Can we go somewhere else and sit down?"

"You're right." Fern put an arm around me and hoisted me up. "There are too many stiffs in this room."

We walked gingerly out to the lobby, and I sank into a blue wing-back chair.

"How long was I out?"

"It couldn't have been very long," Fern said. "You only got here twenty minutes ago. Lucky for me I happened to come out into the hall right after Barbie screamed."

"Botox Barbie found me?" So that was the high-pitched shrieking I'd heard. The woman had some lungs on her.

"She said she was on her way to the ladies' room when she saw the door standing open and your feet sticking out."

"There you are." Richard rushed up to us with Kate close on his heels. They both looked about five shades paler than usual. "The next time you get attacked, try not to wander off. I lost a year off my life."

Kate pressed a hand to her mouth. "Are you okay?"

"I'm fine, I think," I said. "It probably looks worse than it is."

Richard looked at my head. "I certainly hope so."

"What happened?" Kate took a seat in the matching wing-back chair next to me.

"I was headed to the ladies' room to get more tissues for Lucille and I saw an open viewing room with the lights out."

Richard rolled his eyes. "And you took that as an invitation to go inside? Have you never seen a horror movie, Annabelle?"

"I was curious to see if they keep bodies in all of these rooms. Otherwise where would they keep all the caskets before the services?"

Fern glanced around him. "Do you really think there are corpses in all of these rooms?"

Richard tapped his foot on the floor. "Go on."

"I was looking for the light switch when the door slammed shut on me."

"What a surprise," Richard muttered.

"Do you want me to continue?" I asked.

Richard pursed his lips. I could tell that he was torn between the desire to give me a proper scolding and the desire to hear my story. "By all means."

"I opened the door to leave when I was hit on the head by something hard." My hand instinctively went to the tender spot.

Fern gasped. "Someone was in the room with you?"

"No, they were in the doorway when I opened

the door to leave. I got blinded for a moment so I only saw an outline of a person. I have no idea who attacked me."

"A bust," Richard said.

"Excuse me?"

"They found one of those god-awful marble busts on the floor between you and Margery. That's what you were hit with."

"Your feet were sticking outside the room, but Margery lay inside next to the bust," Fern said. "It looks like Margery saw your feet and came in the room, then got attacked as well."

"So whoever hit me must have still been inside the room when Margery came in," I said. "Do you know if she's okay?"

"I'm sure they'll be fine," Kate said.

"More people were attacked than me and Margery?" I asked.

"Not really," Richard explained. "When Lucille saw Margery she fainted and hit the ground pretty hard."

"Poor Lucille," I said. "I don't know how much more she can take."

Fern pulled out his handkerchief. "I don't know how much more any of us can take. This week has been a wedding planner bloodbath."

"This is getting too dangerous for my taste," Kate agreed. "Next time you might not be so lucky, Annie."

I bit the edge of my lip. "But we're getting so close to the killer. I can feel it."

"That's your head you're feeling, honey." Fern patted my arm.

Richard gaped at me. "You don't honestly plan

on continuing to hunt for this serial killer your-self, do you?"

"I'm not hunting for him. I'm gathering infor-mation."

"What if the killer knows about your little in-formation gathering project and tried to get rid of you so you won't get any closer to finding him?" Richard asked. "Did you think of that?"

"You don't think this was another random wedding planner murder?" Kate said. "You think the killer targeted Annabelle because she knows too much?"

"Someone had to watch her go in the viewing room and then follow her with the marble bust," Richard said. "I don't think any of these murders are random. Especially not this one."

"That means that the killer probably knows that we were all poking around for information," Kate said, looking a bit green. "He could come af-ter any of us next."

"Lots of people knew that we were asking questions about the murders," I said. "Remem-ber that both Barbie and Gail mentioned hearing about it?"

"Must you run around advertising what you're doing all the time?" Richard asked me. "Is your investigation really worth one of our lives?"

I opened my mouth to defend myself, but tears pricked the back of my eyes. Richard was right. I couldn't risk my life or anyone else's looking for the killer. I would never forgive myself if some-thing happened to one of my friends.

"I'm sorry." My voice cracked. "I never thought that I was putting us in danger."

"That's okay, honey." Fern squeezed my hand. "No harm done." His eyes darted to my head. "Well, almost no harm."

Richard fixed me with a serious look. "Will you promise to leave the detective work to the detectives from now on?"

I held up my hand, palm out. "I give you my word."

"What a relief." Richard sighed. "I thought you were going to put up a big fight."

A nagging voice in the back of my head told me that I already had all the information I needed to find the killer. Putting the pieces together could hardly be called detective work, I reasoned with myself. What harm could come from thinking about the case?

I shook my head. "You don't have to worry about me. I'm hanging up my detective hat for good." Not really a lie, I thought. More like an omission.

Chapter 25

"I'm calling to get the scoop," I said, sinking down onto my couch holding the phone to my ear with one hand and an ice pack to my head with the other. I'd convinced Kate and Richard that I was fine by myself and had scooted them out the door so I could do some armchair investigating in peace.

I knew Richard was right. I would never forgive myself if something happened to one of my friends because the killer thought we were poking around too close. But I could also never live with myself if more people died and I could do something to stop it. I just had to keep a low profile from now on. Catching up on industry gossip with Joni was the best way I could think of to find out everything that was going on without leaving my couch.

"Annabelle?" Joni sounded surprised. "I thought they took you to the hospital along with Margery and Lucille."

"No. I'm fine. A doctor took a look at me but let me come home to rest."

"Do you need someone to check on you?"

"Fern promised to stop by after he goes to Eleanor's memorial service this afternoon."

Joni sighed. "I'm glad I don't have to video that one, too. One a day is plenty for me. Was Fern close to Eleanor?"

"No, he just loves the drama. He would have been a great professional mourner. He can cry at the drop of a hat."

"That may come in handy. Eleanor didn't have any family that I've ever heard of and she drove everyone she worked with crazy."

"She drove you nuts, too?" I rearranged myself on the couch. "I thought it was just other wedding planners she annoyed."

"Imagine hearing that you're going to be doing a million dollar wedding for a major celebrity and then getting to the job and finding out the celebrity is the weather guy for Channel 7."

I cringed. "That's bad."

"No kidding. And if that wedding cost a million dollars then I'm Steven Spielberg."

I laughed then felt guilty about making fun of Eleanor. After all, she had been murdered.

"But I can't imagine that someone killed her because she lied her head off," I said.

"No, me either. I've been pushed to the edge by wedding planners before but I've never killed one of them."

"Are we really that bad?" I knew what I thought of some of my colleagues but it was always interesting to hear what other vendors thought.

"Not you, of course," Joni said quickly. "Or the other newer planners like Stephanie. But don't get me going about the ones that think they're practically celebrities themselves like Byron and Gail."

"I guess Byron is a bit high maintenance."

"Are you kidding me?" Joni was starting to get worked up. "I've done weddings for thirteen hours where Byron and Gail forgot to feed any of the vendors but set up a table with china and crystal for themselves and had the waiter serve them filet mignon along with the guests."

My mouth dropped open. "You're kidding." I felt guilty if I didn't join the other wedding vendors in the usual offering of limp club sandwiches. "I've never seen that side of them."

"Trust me, Annabelle. If they think you can't do anything for them, they don't even give you the time of day. But I've had the last laugh. They have no idea how many brides I've steered away from them since that wedding."

"Really?" I swallowed hard and made a mental note never to tick off Joni.

"Sure. Lots of brides ask me my opinion on planners and I give it to them."

"So what do you think about the murders?" I tried to change the subject and see if Joni had heard anything I hadn't. "Who do you think could be out to kill wedding planners?"

"Take your pick on who wanted Carolyn and Eleanor dead, but there's only one person I know who had a motive to kill Stephanie."

I held my breath. "Who?"

"Guess who Maxwell Gray had been referring

some of his brides to?" Joni didn't wait for me to guess. "Stephanie Burke."

"Stephanie was getting business from Maxwell?"

"Either they were involved or he was hoping that they would be," Joni said. "Either way, he was giving business to Stephanie and not to some of the other planners that he used to be involved with."

"Like Carolyn and Eleanor?"

"And like Gail. I heard that she was pretty upset about it."

I snapped my fingers. "You're right. I saw her fighting with Maxwell at his party right before Stephanie was found dead."

"There you go. I wouldn't put it past Gail to whack Stephanie in a jealous rage or to do it to protect her business."

I sat up and put my ice bag on the coffee table. "That would explain why Gail was so eager to set Byron up to take the fall. She must be trying to divert attention away from herself. But would she really murder someone out of jealousy?"

"I'd be careful if I were you, Annabelle. These people are as dangerous as they are obsessive-compulsive. I wouldn't put it past them to have a prioritized to-do list for the murders."

"Don't worry, Joni. After today, I'm going to lay low. I've had as much drama as I can take for one day."

Fern burst through my front door and held up what looked like a small gray urn. "You are never going to believe what I got from Eleanor Applebaum's funeral."

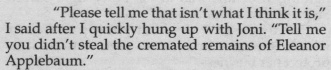

Chapter 26

"Please tell me that isn't what I think it is," I said after I quickly hung up with Joni. "Tell me you didn't steal the cremated remains of Eleanor Applebaum."

Fern recoiled in mock horror. "Of course not." He put the small urn down on my coffee table. "These were the favors."

"There were favors at a funeral?"

Fern shrugged. "It was a funeral for a wedding planner. I have to admit it seemed a bit like a wedding. The programs had gold tassels, there was a string quartet, and we all signed a big picture of Eleanor instead of a guest book. Do you have anything to drink, darling?"

"In the kitchen." I pointed without getting up. "So who was at the funeral?"

"Not as many people as were at Carolyn's viewing but a decent turnout."

"The way wedding planners are dropping, can you really blame people for not showing?" I called over my shoulder. "Anything good happen?"

"Nothing as juicy as your little drama earlier, of course. I could have sworn I saw Gail and Byron arrive together, but they made a point to avoid each other. Maxwell made an appearance but even he looked somber. His shirt was buttoned up all the way."

"Why would Gail and Byron arrive together and then pretend not to know each other?"

"I could have been mistaken or they could just be that moody to speak to each other one minute then hate each other the next. You should have seen the decor for this shindig."

"I heard that Eleanor didn't have any family," I said. "Who put it all together?"

"She must have left specific instructions because it was beautifully planned. I've never seen such breathtaking flowers at a memorial service. All in shades of pink. And I could swear she brought in specialty lighting."

"How odd. It does sound like a wedding." I picked up the miniature urn. "But why would someone give away little urns as favors at a funeral? It's a bit macabre."

"How else could they give everyone some of Eleanor's ashes to take home?" Fern called from the kitchen. "Little plastic baggies would be gauche and the ashes would fall through tulle sachets."

I screamed and almost dropped the urn. "Eleanor's ashes are in here?" I carefully put the urn back on the table and started wiping my hands on the couch. "I thought you said you didn't have her ashes."

"I said I didn't *steal* her ashes." Fern walked

back in the room with a glass of wine. "They gave them to me."

I shuddered. "Are you telling me that Eleanor's ashes were divided up and given to every guest who attended the memorial service?"

Fern sat next to me and gave me a nudge. "I'll bet you wish you came with me now, don't you?" He took a sip of wine. "Not everyone got them but I elbowed my way to the front before they all got snatched up."

"Good thing," I said, averting my glance from where Eleanor sat on my coffee table. "What are you going to do with it?"

Fern raised an eyebrow. "I don't know. Do you want it? You could use it as a bud vase."

"Not the urn." I tried to keep my voice even. "What are you going to do with the ashes?"

Fern made a face. "I hadn't thought that far." He looked around my apartment.

"Don't even think it," I said. "You're going to have to take her with you."

Fern gasped. "After I go to all the trouble to bring you back a present from the funeral, this is how I'm treated?"

I folded my arms and leveled my gaze at Fern. "Not bad."

Fern let out a sigh. "Do you really think so? I wasn't a bit much? Should I have teared up?"

"No, it was good. The tears would have been over the top," I reassured him. "But you're still taking her with you."

Fern put down his wine and picked up Eleanor. "Fine. I'd better go find something to do with her and get ready for tomorrow."

"Isn't tomorrow only Friday?" I asked, hoping I hadn't lost track of the days. "The wedding is on Saturday."

"You may not have to work tomorrow but I have to do the bride and her mother for the rehearsal dinner." Fern groaned. "You know how picky Kitty and Lady are about their hair. I've blocked out the entire afternoon at the salon."

"I have to admit that for once I'm looking forward to a wedding." I stood and walked with Fern to the door. "After the past few days, a wedding will be calm in comparison. We haven't had a single meltdown by the bride or one middle-of-the-night phone call from the M.O.B. It should be smooth sailing."

Fern tapped the miniature urn on my door frame as he walked out and gave me a wink. "Knock on wood."

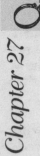

Chapter 27

"Are you sure this is such a good idea?" Kate asked as I handed her the gift basket to be delivered to the Hay-Adams Hotel.

I followed her from my office to the front door of my apartment. "The mother of the groom requested a bottle of Jameson's Irish whiskey to be delivered to the priest's room before he arrived. I'm just following orders."

"It's a huge bottle." Kate shifted her weight to balance the basket on her hip, which barely held up her low-rider jeans. "This basket weighs a ton."

"Are you sure you don't mind doing the errands for the Winchester wedding?"

"You shouldn't be driving around after what happened yesterday at Carolyn's viewing. The only other thing I have to do is inventory the rentals at the hotel. Once I drop this at the front desk, I'll do a quick count to make sure everything is there, then come back and pick you up for the rehearsal."

"Thanks, Kate." I opened the door for her. "I'm going to stay here and make the final changes to the timeline. Call me if you need anything."

She looked back as she started down the stairs. "You're sure you're going to stay here and keep out of trouble?"

"After what happened yesterday?" I gave her a shocked look. "Trust me. I'm looking forward to a quiet day."

I closed the door after her and walked to the kitchen. I opened the refrigerator and scanned the bare shelves. A few cans of Diet Dr Pepper sat next to some cartons of leftover Chinese food. I took a can of soda and popped it open. Breakfast of champions. I started down the hall to my office but was stopped by my doorbell.

"Hold on a sec," I called as I went back and opened the front door, expecting to see Kate. "What did you forget?"

Instead Ian stood on my doorstep in snug jeans and his leather jacket zipped halfway over a black T-shirt.

"I just got your message this morning," Ian said, his brows furrowed. "My cell phone has been acting up. Are you sure you're okay?"

I'd almost forgotten that I'd called him after my run-in at the funeral parlor. I wasn't sure why I'd felt the need to call him, but I felt better already just from seeing him. "I'm fine. It was nothing really."

He stepped closer to me and lifted a hand to my head, brushing his fingertips lightly over my bruise. His blue eyes met mine. "It doesn't look like nothing."

"The doctor said that since most of the force landed on the side of my head, it didn't cause any major trauma."

Ian cocked an eyebrow. "You're speaking American again."

I smiled. "If someone tried to kill me, they missed."

"I don't like the idea of someone trying to kill you, even if they missed." Ian frowned. "You need to be more careful."

"I can take care of myself." I tried to keep the irritation out of my voice. "You could have called me back, you know. You didn't have to rush over here to check on me."

"If I called, you might get irritated at me like you are now and not let me bring you breakfast." He held out a white paper bag. "That, and we have to leave for a gig later today, so if I didn't see you now, I might not see you for a couple of days. I wasn't sure if I could last that long."

I felt my pulse quicken and my anger melt away. "Oh." I stepped back to let him inside and focused on the paper bag so I wouldn't have to meet his eyes. "Bagels?"

He shook his head. "Chocolate croissants from Patisserie Poupon."

My stomach growled instinctively. "My favorite. How did you know?"

Ian smiled. "I have my ways."

He followed me into the kitchen and unpacked the contents of the paper bag on the counter, peeling the pastries from sheets of white translucent paper. I handed him a can of Diet Dr Pepper from the refrigerator.

"It's all I have," I said. "You should probably know that I don't keep a well-stocked pantry."

He grinned as he took the can from me. "That means we'll have to go out a lot."

I felt my cheeks begin to flush. "That doesn't sound so bad."

He handed me a flaky chocolate croissant. "Good. I hoped it wouldn't."

I took a bite and had to stop myself from moaning out loud. The combination of the buttery pastry and the rich chocolate was heavenly. Ian moved close to me and tilted my chin up toward him. I held my breath as he brushed my lips with his fingertips.

"You have bits of croissant on your lips," he whispered, his face only inches above mine. He leaned down and his lips met mine so gently I almost couldn't tell he was kissing me except for the heat that surged through my body. I sunk into the kiss as he wrapped his arms around me and buried his hands in my hair. I dropped my croissant on the counter and lifted my arms to encircle his neck. He pressed his body against mine and his kiss became deeper and more urgent.

"Annabelle!"

It took me a moment to realize that it wasn't Ian who called out my name. It was Leatrice. I sprang back from Ian as I heard her come into my apartment. When would I remember to lock my door?

"In the kitchen," I yelled, straightening my shirt.

Ian reached over and brushed my lips with his thumb. "You still have crumbs," he said softly.

I smiled at him and noticed that his eyes burned

with heat. For the first time he looked dangerous to me. I took a breath to compose myself as Leatrice bounded into the kitchen.

"There you are, dearie." She saw Ian and her face lit up. "I didn't know you were visiting, too."

"I brought breakfast." Ian motioned to the croissants abandoned on the counter.

Leatrice rubbed her hands together. "Shall we take them to the dining room table and have a proper breakfast?"

Ian glanced at his watch. "I actually should be going. We have to head down to Charlottesville for a gig tonight and the lads will kill me if I don't help them load the truck."

Leatrice's smile drooped. "Can't you stay for a while? I wanted to tell you all the things I heard on the police scanner this morning. Tonight is a full moon, you know. People go crazy when there's a full moon."

"I'll be back on Saturday," he said more to me than Leatrice. "Can we pick up where we left off?"

I felt my cheeks get red and started to nod when I remembered the Winchester wedding. "I can't. I have a wedding at The Hay-Adams on Saturday."

"How about Sunday?"

"It's a date," I said, walking Ian to the door with Leatrice close on my heels.

Ian opened the door and stepped into the hall. He gave me a lingering kiss on the cheek and waved at Leatrice.

"See you on Sunday," she called out, waving as he disappeared down the stairs.

I turned to Leatrice once we'd gone back in my apartment. "What are you wearing?"

She spun around and the bright red felt skirt belled out around her. The skirt was decorated with vividly colored sequined appliqués of nutcrackers, angels, and wrapped presents. "It's called a Christmas tree skirt. Do you like it?"

"You're wearing a Christmas tree skirt?"

Leatrice looked at me like I was an idiot. "Well, it is the Christmas season. This is a very popular item on the Home Shopping Network. I'm sure you'll see other people wearing them around."

"I doubt it." I didn't have the heart to break it to her that the skirt was meant to wrap around the base of a Christmas tree. At least she was in season.

Leatrice stared at me for a second. "Why do you have crumbs in your hair, dear?"

My cheeks burned as I ran my hands vigorously through my hair to get rid of the croissant crumbs that Ian had obviously left behind.

Leatrice's eyes bugged out. "And what happened to your head?"

"I had an accident." I tried to be as vague as possible. "Nothing serious."

Leatrice sank onto my sofa. "Did you fall?"

"Not exactly," I confessed.

"You mean someone did that to you?" She clapped her hand over her mouth. "I knew I should have stayed with you and been your bodyguard."

Luckily, my cell phone rang before Leatrice could ask me any more questions. I grabbed it off my coffee table and flipped it open.

"Wedding Belles. This is—"

"Annabelle, it's Lady Margaret Winchester." I'd never heard Lady in a rush before. "Could you do me a huge favor? We need someone to pick up the priest from the airport and take him to the church for the rehearsal."

"Sure," I agreed, grabbing a pen and writing the flight information down on the back of a nearby magazine. I was glad Kate wasn't around to see me caving in to a client's last minute request again. "I'll be there."

"You're a lifesaver," Lady said. "I'm running to have my tiara refitted, but call my cell if you need me."

I'd never heard of a tiara fitting, but nothing brides did surprised me anymore. I snapped my phone shut.

Leatrice stood with the door opened. "You're in no condition to drive with that welt on your head so consider me your wheel man."

I sighed, too tired to argue about it. My nice, quite afternoon had officially been shot to hell.

Chapter 28

"You're sure you don't want to take my car?" I asked as we got in Leatrice's yellow Ford Fairmont circa 1980-something. I could only imagine the impression we would make on the priest by driving up in a car as long as a school bus with an eighty-year-old driver sitting on a pile of phone books and wearing a pair of prescription flying goggles.

"Not when we've got a classic car at our disposal." Leatrice rubbed the dashboard and a cloud of dust surrounded us. I think she confused old with classic. I knew that when my brides requested a classic car for their wedding they meant a pristine Rolls-Royce, not a car with sagging interior fabric and missing door handles.

"This baby purrs like a kitten." Leatrice put the key in the ignition, and the motor rumbled to life with a violent grinding sound. Leatrice had clearly never heard a kitten purr.

She didn't bother to look behind her as she

pulled out from the two spaces on the street that her car took up. It had been no use trying to convince her that the trip would be boring, and I hadn't been fast enough to lose her on the stairs.

"This is so exciting." Leatrice clapped her hands as we drove through Georgetown. "A day in the life of a wedding planner."

"Being a wedding planner is far from exciting, Leatrice. Most days I make phone calls and work with contracts. Yesterday was not the norm."

Holiday wreaths hung from every streetlight, and signs proclaiming sales hung in each shop window in the fashionable Washington neighborhood. Delivery trucks and double-parked cars didn't make it any easier to weave our way through the usual gridlock and impatient holiday shoppers. Having a car longer than most of the delivery trucks also seemed to be a drawback.

Leatrice turned around in her seat to face me while we stopped to let a group of tourists cross the street. Her eyes looked enormous through her prescription goggles. "You haven't told me what happened yesterday."

Oops. "I assumed you'd heard on your police scanner."

"Heard what? Did I miss something big?" She practically bounced out of her seat as she thumped herself on the forehead. "I knew I should have gotten a second scanner for the bathroom. I try to be quick but I lose precious moments in the shower."

"It wasn't a big deal in the end." I tried to gloss over the attempted murders in the hope that she wouldn't get all worked up about them. "A couple more wedding planners were attacked, but no one ended up dying."

"The police think it was the same perp?" Leatrice used law enforcement jargon as much as possible.

I held my breath as we swung onto M Street and veered onto Key Bridge without signaling. "A slightly different weapon, but they're assuming it's the same person."

Leatrice rapped her fingers on the steering wheel. "The first two victims were both strangled. What did he use this time?"

"Three victims," I corrected her. "A third wedding planner was strangled at an industry party Wednesday night."

Leatrice gasped. "I can't believe I missed that, too. This is awful. I'm definitely going to get a second scanner. So how were the latest victims attacked?"

"I guess there wasn't anything in the funeral home to choke someone with so the killer used a marble bust."

"Blunt force trauma instead of asphyxiation. Curious." Leatrice looked at my bruise and narrowed her eyes at me. "Were you one of the people to get attacked?"

"Technically yes," I said. "But I didn't get hit very hard. I'm fine."

"Does Detective Reese know about this?" Leatrice reached over and opened the glove compartment, then pulled out a cell phone that looked as old as her car.

"Of course. He showed up at the funeral parlor and questioned everyone," I said, hanging on to the door handle as we took the exit for the GW Parkway toward the airport. I glanced at the cell phone as Leatrice put it back in the glove compartment. "Is that a rotary dial?"

"Does he think you're in danger?"

"He warned me to be careful." Actually, he'd threatened to throw me in jail if I came within ten feet of the murder investigation, but Leatrice didn't need specifics.

She gave a low whistle. "So that's three people who have been murdered—all wedding planners—plus two more wedding planners almost killed."

"I wouldn't say that I was almost killed," I said. "The other victim fared worse than I did. They admitted her to the hospital for a possible concussion." I made a mental note to call the hospital and check on Margery later.

"This may be the first wedding planner serial killer in the history of violent crime." Leatrice looked positively gleeful. "I wonder who would want to kill a bunch of wedding planners?"

"A bride?" I guessed. "Although it should be the other way around."

"Do you have any suspects?" she asked as we drove along the Potomac River. Without leaves on the trees, it was even easier to see the stark white marble of the city's monuments reflected in the water. The river looked like a sheet of gray glass today without the usual crowd of boats that packed the water during the warmer months.

I hesitated for a moment, but talking with Leatrice about the suspects seemed harmless enough.

"The first two victims are both older planners who have a lot of connections to each other. They actually had plenty of reasons to kill each other," I said. "When it comes to motives, Carolyn's husband stood to gain the most financially, but no one saw him at the crime scene and he doesn't have any reason to kill the other victims. Several people could have killed Carolyn as revenge for being fired. Byron, Gail, and two sales clerks were all fired by Carolyn and weren't too happy about it."

"It sounds like the first victim wasn't the most loved planner in town," Leatrice said.

"Nope. She'd been around forever, but she'd also had lots of time to make enemies."

"What about the other old-timer?" Bold words coming from someone who had the distinctive scent of Ben-Gay.

"Eleanor was more annoying than anything. Someone could have killed her so they wouldn't have to hear her bragging about her fancy clients anymore. She took part in firing Byron, so he wasn't a big fan of hers, either."

"So they had Byron in common?" Leatrice said.

"And Maxwell. I always forget him. They both had affairs with him when they were all a lot younger. Actually, Carolyn used Eleanor's affair to blackmail her into leaving the company."

Leatrice's eyes widened. "I imagined wedding planners being so prim and proper."

I laughed. "Guess again."

"What about the third victim?"

"Stephanie didn't have much in common with the other two at all. She was young and new and everyone liked her," I said. "Well, the old guard may not have liked her, but they don't like anyone new. I can't figure out why anyone would kill Stephanie."

"She didn't have anything in common with Carolyn or Eleanor?" Leatrice pressed.

I gnawed the edge of my lower lip. "She got friendly with Maxwell at the party before she was murdered, but I have a hard time thinking someone killed her because of that. Even if they were jealous."

"It sounds like it's the one thing that links them all together, though." Leatrice hunted around in her glove compartment with one hand. "I wish I had something to write all this down on."

"Shouldn't you concentrate on the road?" I asked as we drove under the highway and swerved into the right lane. We were making record time to the airport. Probably because Leatrice either couldn't read the speed limit signs or didn't care about them. "But I was never involved with Maxwell and neither was Margery."

Leatrice snapped the glove compartment closed. "Margery?"

"The other wedding planner who got attacked at the funeral home," I explained. "Carolyn's assistant."

"So she probably had the same connections to Eleanor and the other planners who had it in for Carolyn?"

"She'd worked for Carolyn for almost twenty years, so she knew them all and worked either for them or with them. But nobody held Carolyn's actions against Margery. She was only her assistant.

And I didn't have an affair with Maxwell or a history of working with the same people that Carolyn and Eleanor did, so who knows why I was targeted?"

"My guess would be that the killer wanted to keep you from poking around in the case."

"That's what Richard and Reese think," I admitted.

"Those are all the suspects and clues? No photos or video footage?" Leatrice looked dismayed when I shook my head. "There's not much to go on."

"Well, we know that Byron lied about leaving the Mayflower for the church when he really stayed at the hotel where Carolyn was killed." I spotted the yellow and white terminal on my left and motioned for Leatrice to take the first exit for Ronald Reagan National Airport.

"That's pretty incriminating. How did you find out?"

I unfolded the piece of paper where I'd written down the flight information. "Gail. She and Byron work together a lot."

"The same Gail who got fired by Carolyn? Are you sure she isn't telling you to set him up and make herself look good?"

I directed Leatrice to the arrivals section of the airport complex. "I'm not sure of anything and I wouldn't put it past her. She and Byron are supposed to be friends, but she ratted him out to us. And I'm not so sure they aren't still friends."

"Some friend," Leatrice said. "Who do you think would be capable of strangling three people?"

"I'd say Byron if I didn't think he was too prissy

to pull it off. Gail is vicious enough to do it, but I'm not sure of her motive to kill Margery or me even if she was jealous enough of Stephanie to commit murder. If the victims were strangled in some sort of autoerotic asphyxiation, I'd bet money on Maxwell. But I really don't see him as a murderer."

Leatrice cocked her head to one side. "Auto what?"

"Nothing important." I didn't relish the idea of explaining S&M to Leatrice. "My point is that I have plenty of suspects but no idea who really did it."

Leatrice swung the car in front of the baggage claim entrance and slammed it into park.

"Wait here. I'll be right back," I said as I hopped out of the car. "All I have to do is find an Irish priest."

"Will any Irish priest do, lassie?" A stocky man with a head full of bushy white hair called out in a thick accent.

I stopped and turned around. "Are you Father O'Malley?"

"Aye." He picked up his slightly battered suitcase from the curb. "I'm here for the Kelly-Winchester wedding."

I gave a sigh of relief. I'd found the priest. Now I just had to deliver him safely to the wedding rehearsal. This should be a breeze.

"I'm Annabelle Archer. The wedding planner."

"A wedding planner? They hired you to plan their wedding?" The priest scratched his head. "How marvelous!"

"The car is right here."

Father O'Malley's eyes widened when he saw

the yellow stretch Ford. Leatrice leaned out and waved as she popped the trunk. I helped him hoist his suitcase inside, then opened the front passenger side door for him and jumped in the back.

Father O'Malley lowered himself into the passenger's side and gave a start when he saw Leatrice. "Are you a wedding planner, too, young lady?"

Leatrice giggled and I rolled my eyes. Pretty suave for a priest.

"I'm her neighbor and driver." She held out her hand. "Leatrice Butters. You can call me Lee Lee."

My mouth almost hit the ground. Lee Lee? This was new. "Leatrice, this is the *priest* for tomorrow's wedding. We're taking him to the church for the wedding rehearsal."

"Do we have some time to spare?" Father O'Malley looked back at me.

"A bit," I said, pointing Leatrice to the exit heading back into the city. "Would you like a driving tour of the monuments?"

"I hoped we could stop somewhere for a pint before going to the church."

"A pint of what?" I couldn't imagine wanting ice cream in weather like this. I glanced at the ruddy-cheeked priest. "Do you mean you want to stop for a drink?" He looked like he'd already had a few.

"You do have pubs in Washington, don't you?"

Leatrice's face lit up. "Oh yes, let's go to a pub. I've never been to one."

The priest turned and winked at me. "That's a good girl."

I rubbed my temples as I imagined what Kitty would say when I showed up at the rehearsal with an inebriated priest. I didn't even want to think about arriving in an ancient Ford driven by an equally ancient driver in a sequined Christmas tree skirt.

The murder investigation had just become the least of my worries.

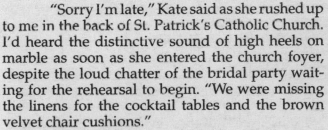

Chapter 29

"Sorry I'm late," Kate said as she rushed up to me in the back of St. Patrick's Catholic Church. I'd heard the distinctive sound of high heels on marble as soon as she entered the church foyer, despite the loud chatter of the bridal party waiting for the rehearsal to begin. "We were missing the linens for the cocktail tables and the brown velvet chair cushions."

"Did you call the rental company?" I rubbed my arms to keep warm. Kate had changed from her jeans into a short black dress with a deep scoop neck. It made me cold just looking at her.

"They're sending the stuff over first thing in the morning. How's the rehearsal going so far?"

"We have most of the bridal party here." I cast a glance around at the blond bridesmaids and the tall, dark groomsmen. The combination of a Texas-Irish wedding produced a very attractive bridal party. "All we need is a bride and we'll be good to go."

"A bride running late for the rehearsal? What a surprise." Kate craned her neck around me and peered into the sanctuary. The lights were dimmed and the sanctuary was illuminated by the glow of chandeliers hanging above the rows of dark wooden pews. The church was almost a miniature cathedral with a towering domed ceiling and ornate stained-glass windows throughout. An enormous crucifix hung over the alabaster marble altar table, and the cross reflected in the high sheen of the aisle.

"Wait until you hear what I found out at the Hay-Adams...Um, Annabelle. Is that Leatrice sitting in the back row?"

I gave a tiny nod without looking her in the eyes.

"What is she doing here?"

I put a hand to my head and began to massage in small circles. "Don't ask. I spent the last hour in a bar with an Irish priest and an eighty-year-old."

"Excuse me?" Kate's eyebrows disappeared under her blond bangs. "All you have to do now is get yourself a duck and a rabbi and you'll be set."

I glared at her. "You're a riot."

"Leatrice at a bar? I didn't even know she drank."

"She doesn't." I motioned with my head as Leatrice began to slide lower in the pew. "That's part of the problem."

Kate looked around the foyer. "Where's the priest you went bar-hopping with?"

"Shhhhh." I motioned for her to lower her voice. "He's back in the sacristy with the monsignor. You'd never know he downed three beers in an hour aside from the slightly slurred speech. But that may just be his accent. I can't really tell."

Kate's mouth fell open. "Wasn't the bride's mother worried about people drinking at the wedding?"

"I'm sure she didn't think she'd have to worry about the priest," I said.

"This should be an exciting rehearsal."

"To say the least." I glanced nervously around the foyer for Kitty. "What did you want to tell me about the Hay-Adams?"

"I got a chance to talk to David, the catering director, while I inventoried the rentals."

"The one who calls you 'babe'?"

Kate smiled. What I might consider sexist, Kate took as a compliment. "Exactly. He mentioned that they had a nice wedding last Saturday with one of our colleagues."

"Who?"

"None other than our Botox poster girl."

"Barbie?" I said. "So she was working right around the corner from us."

"Not only that," Kate continued. "Did you know that Barbie wasn't as friendly with Carolyn as she liked people to think? Barbie begged her for a job once when she was between husbands and Carolyn turned her down and hired someone else just to be mean."

My mouth fell open. The Hay-Adams stood only blocks away from the Mayflower Hotel. Barbie could have jumped in a cab and made it to the Mayflower and back before anyone would have missed her.

Kate waved her hands. "Wait, there's more. Did you know that Barbie's latest husband is loaded, and she bragged to David about her husband buying her something really big that people would be stunned by?"

"Like her lips?"

Kate gave me an exasperated sigh. "Like a business? Like the Wedding Shoppe?"

"She said that?"

"No," Kate said. "I came up with that on my own. But it's a possibility, don't you think?"

There was a greater possibility that the "big" surprise Barbie got so excited about involved some sort of plastic surgery, but I hated to burst Kate's bubble.

"Did David notice her missing during their wedding last Saturday?" I asked.

"He said that she went out for a smoke a few times and stayed outside for a while."

"In this weather? I didn't know that Barbie smoked, did you?"

"No, but Barbie and I aren't real tight," Kate said. "She could be one of those secret smokers."

I reluctantly agreed. "It would explain the voice."

"Didn't Barbie find you and Marjorie at the funeral home?" Kate lowered her voice. "Maybe she found you because she's the one who attacked you."

I shivered. "Fern did say that he walked out in the hall right after Barbie found us. What if she claimed to have discovered our bodies when really she hadn't had time to leave the crime scene before Fern saw her? I can understand that she hated Carolyn, but what does she have against me or Marjorie?"

"Or Eleanor and Stephanie, for that matter?" Kate said. "I guess it's not a great theory after all."

"Annabelle, Kate." Kitty Winchester's face barely peeked above the thick collar of her gray fox coat as she flounced through the sea of bridesmaids and groomsmen to reach us. "Just who I needed to see."

"Is Lady with you?" Kate asked.

"Well, yes." Kitty motioned behind her to the only blonde covered from head to toe in a white fur coat. "But we have a bit of an emergency."

My breath caught in my throat. Wedding emergencies weren't good.

"We left the flower girl's basket back in Texas. Could you find us a new one by tomorrow?"

I let out a breath. This wasn't an emergency. A real emergency consisted of sending the grandmothers off to the wrong wedding or a bride's veil getting flushed down a toilet. This was a tiny blip on the wedding radar screen and was nothing we couldn't handle.

"No problem," I said. "I can even get one that matches the guest book and ring bearer's pillow."

Kitty pressed a hand to her throat, and then looked past us to the altar. "I'm so relieved. Now I should go introduce myself to the priest since he flew in all the way from Ireland."

"This should be interesting," Kate said as Kitty flounced down the aisle.

I glanced down at my watch. "I'm going to run to the Wedding Shoppe and get the flower girl basket before the store closes."

"You're leaving me to run the rehearsal?" Kate asked, her voice edged with panic.

"The priest will run it," I reassured her. "All you have to do is line people up."

"I thought you said the priest was drunk."

I held up a finger. "I said he *may* be drunk. I can't tell for sure."

"What about Leatrice?" Kate jerked a thumb in the direction of Leatrice's head, barely visible above the pew and sinking lower every second.

"Make sure she doesn't mingle with people," I said. "She's wearing a Christmas tree skirt."

Kate folded her arms across her chest. "I don't even know what that is, but if Leatrice is wearing it I'm assuming it's weird."

"I promise I'll be back before you can even miss me," I said, backing out of the foyer toward the main doors of the church.

"The pathway to hell is lined with good inventions," Kate grumbled.

Chapter 30

"Hello!" I pushed open the front door to the Wedding Shoppe and stepped inside, grateful they were still open and glad to be out of the frigid weather. I pulled off my gloves and laid them on a nearby table that was stacked with colorful wedding planning guides. "Is anyone here?"

Lucille appeared from the back of the shop. "Can I help you?" Her face softened when she saw me. "Oh, Annabelle, it's you."

"Sorry to be coming in right before you close on a Friday night, but we have a bit of a flower girl emergency." My eyes scanned wall shelves that were crowded with glittering white wedding accessories. Everything from purses to garters to photo albums filled the store from end to end. "The wedding is tomorrow and the bride's mother forgot the flower girl basket."

Lucille smiled, and she looked better than she had in days. "If there's anyone who understands a wedding crisis, it's me. Where's the wedding?"

"The ceremony is at St. Patrick's, the cocktail reception is at the Hay-Adams, and the dinner and dancing are at the Decatur House."

"I love the Hay-Adams. Are you using the roof?"

I nodded. "We're bringing in tons of heaters since it will be so cold, but the bride had to have guests overlooking the White House for cocktails."

"It is the best view in the city." Lucille had a faraway look in her eyes. "I'm sure it will be beautiful with all the holiday decorations up. What are the bride's colors?"

"Chocolate brown and mint green. She didn't want to get too Christmasy, but she wanted colors that fit the season. I just hope we all don't freeze to death outside in this weather." I rubbed my hands together to warm them up. "So do you have a flower girl basket in the Liberace collection?"

"Is the bride from South Florida?" Lucille asked as she led me to the shelf with the heavily beaded wedding accessories.

"No, Texas," I said. "Good guess, though."

Lucille giggled. "It's one of our favorite games. We try to guess what collection people will like by how they're dressed when they come in the shop. If they're wearing crystals or peasant skirts they usually go for the Sierra collection, and if they're wearing fancy high heels they go for the Vera Wang."

"What if they're wearing a business suit and old sneakers?"

Lucille winked at me. "The Cherished Moments."

"You seem to be feeling better," I said. "How's Margery doing?"

Lucille's smile faltered for a moment. "Much better. She's been having headaches, so they're keeping her in the hospital for another night to make sure her head injury isn't serious. I'm glad you didn't get hurt too badly, dear."

"Thanks. I was luckier than Margery, I guess."

Lucille's cheeks flushed. "I'm so embarrassed about fainting at the funeral home. People must think I'm a real softie."

"Of course not," I lied. "What a huge shock to see Margery like that. You probably thought she'd been murdered."

Lucille shivered. "I don't know what I'd do without her. She's always been the tough one around here. She would ask for raises from Carolyn for both of us because I was too scared and she stuck up for me with the other planners."

"Were other planners mean to you?" I pulled the clear plastic box that held the Liberace flower girl basket off the shelf.

Lucille pressed her lips together until they turned white, then seemed to remember I was there and relaxed into a vacant smile again. "Some of them considered me a dingbat and never gave me the time of day."

"Really? I never heard that." It didn't surprise me, though. My wedding industry colleagues weren't the most accepting people.

Lucille patted my hand. "Aren't you sweet? You and Kate have always been kind to me. Not like the others."

"Which others?"

Lucille took the boxed flower girl basket from my hands. "Let me open this for you. They tie them in the box pretty tightly. You don't want to be trying to get it out right before the wedding."

Lucille pulled and tugged at the basket as she walked back up toward the register. "Margery is so much better at this than I am," she muttered as she strained against the plastic ties that secured the basket to the box. "I don't have her arm strength."

"Which wedding planners treated you badly, Lucille?" I asked, trying to keep my voice casual.

"The big ones. Gail, Byron, Barbie." She went behind the cash register, produced a pair of scissors and began hacking at the box. I hoped there would be something left of the basket when she finished. "Carolyn didn't help matters by telling people how forgetful and fragile I was. But Carolyn was wrong. I don't forget things. I never forget anything."

I stepped back from Lucille so I wouldn't be in the path of the flying scissors. "The old guard wasn't very nice to anyone, Lucille. Eleanor pretended she didn't remember me the first twenty times we met."

Lucille looked up. "Really? She made comments about me still being Carolyn's assistant after so many years, but she was unpleasant to everyone so I didn't take it too personally."

I wondered if Lucille had taken it personally enough to kill her. I studied the sweet, white-haired lady and wondered if she'd taken things personally enough to kill everyone. I swallowed hard. Maybe Lucille was right, and she wasn't as fragile as everyone thought she was.

"Did Stephanie treat you badly?" I asked.

Lucille pulled the basket free of the box. "Stephanie? What a sweet girl. Reminded me of myself when I first started out in the wedding business. Full of dreams and high hopes." Lucille's smile faded. "At least she didn't have to live long enough to see her dreams disappear like I did. There's nothing worse than that."

Except maybe being strangled by a photographer's cable, I thought. Lucille might not have been fragile, but she didn't seem too mentally balanced, either.

"So how much do I owe you for the basket?" I said, trying to keep my voice from shaking.

Lucille punched in some numbers on the computerized cash register, still holding the scissors in the other hand. "Let's see. With tax it comes to $27.48."

I fumbled in my wallet for my Wedding Belles corporate credit card and slid it across the wooden counter to her.

Lucille swiped the card and handed it back to me. "Do you need a bag?"

I bobbed my head up and down. I'd never even considered that someone as sweet and seemingly innocent as Lucille could be the killer. She certainly seemed to have the motive, or at least she thought she did.

My throat went dry. That meant that she'd tried to kill me as well. She knew I'd been asking around about the murders, and she also knew when I went out into the hall at the funeral home. It would have been easy for her to come find me and hit me over the head.

But why would she attack Margery? Maybe Margery had started to suspect her or knew some incriminating evidence about Lucille. It didn't make me feel any better to know that Lucille was capable of almost murdering her best friend and that I was alone in the store with her.

I hurriedly signed the receipt that Lucille put on the counter and grabbed the handles of the paper bag. "I'd better get back to the rehearsal. I told Kate where I would be, and she's expecting me any minute now."

"Are you okay, Annabelle?" Lucille came around the counter. "You look a little pale."

"I'm fine," I said a little too forcefully as I stepped back toward the door. I had to get out of there so I could tell Kate that we'd been wrong.

Lucille wasn't the most harmless wedding planner in town. She was the most insane. And in this business, that was saying something.

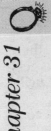

Chapter 31

"Are you sure?" Kate asked as she helped me gather the boxes of programs and favors the bride had left for us at the back of the church. I'd arrived back at the church right after everyone had left for the rehearsal dinner, and Kate was cleaning up. The darkened sanctuary was eerily quiet, and our voices echoed off the marble floors. "I can't imagine Lucille hurting anyone."

"You'd feel differently if you'd heard her talk about how badly the other planners treated her. She held a grudge, that's for sure."

"It gives me the creeps to think that she tried to kill you."

"Tell me about it."

"I wonder why she didn't try again now?" Kate asked. "Was there anyone else in the store?"

"I thought the same thing," I admitted. "Margery hasn't been released from the hospital yet so I know she wasn't there. But there could have been someone in the back that I didn't see. Or maybe Lucille got tired of killing people."

"I can't believe that she tried to kill Margery, too. So much for them being best friends."

"The stress of working together all these years could have gotten to her. Maybe Margery did something that annoyed her and Lucille snapped."

Kate studied me for a moment. "That's comforting."

"I'm not justifying what she did, but maybe she took as much as she could take and finally lost it."

"So what are you going to do?" Kate asked.

"As soon as I get home, I'm calling Detective Reese to tell him everything."

"He's not going to pleased that you went out looking for the killer on your own."

"I went out looking for a flower girl basket," I said. "I just happened to find a deranged killer."

Kate grinned at me. "Do you know how many times I've heard that?"

"Very funny. Okay, I think we have everything," I said, holding a plaid Burberry shopping bag in one hand. "Was this all the bride gave you for tomorrow?"

Kate nodded. "Shouldn't we take Leatrice with us, too?"

I felt like smacking myself on the head. "I completely forgot her." I looked around to the pew where she'd been sitting. "Where did she go?"

"She's still there," Kate said, walking over. "When she slipped all the way down in the pew, I threw my coat over her so no one would see her in that god-awful outfit. Did you know that her skirt has a plug hanging from the back?"

"It lights up?" Only Leatrice wouldn't be deterred by a plug dangling from her clothing.

"It's not very practical, either. You'd have to stand right next to an outlet and not move a lot."

"It's a Christmas tree skirt, Kate," I said. "You're not supposed to wear it."

"Don't worry," Kate said. "You wouldn't catch me dead in it."

I decided not to try to explain the concept of a Christmas tree skirt. "Did the coat hide her?"

I could only imagine how thrilled Kitty would be to have someone passed out during her daughter's wedding rehearsal, much less someone wearing a plug-in skirt. They liked glitz in Texas, but not this kind of glitz.

"No one even knew she was there. Well, except for the snoring."

I groaned. "She snored during the rehearsal?"

"Only a little bit," Kate said. "But once the priest started talking, nobody noticed the snoring."

"I'm afraid to ask."

"It's probably the first wedding rehearsal I've attended where the priest opened with a dirty joke instead of a prayer."

I felt light-headed. If Kitty found out that I took the priest drinking before the rehearsal, she'd have my head. "Did Kitty or Lady say anything?"

"What could they say?" Kate said. "It's the groom's family priest. One side of the church found him hilarious."

"I'm assuming it wasn't the Texas contingent?"

Kate's raised eyebrow was answer enough. "Personally, I can't wait to hear tomorrow's homily."

I pulled the coat off Leatrice and handed it to Kate. "Help me get her to the car."

Kate tugged Leatrice up by one arm. "Come on, sleeping beauty."

"Father O'Malley, you naughty scamp," Leatrice mumbled as I pulled her up from the other side.

Kate almost dropped her. "Did she say what I think she said?"

"Yes, Leatrice has a crush on the priest. Now could we keep moving, please?"

"This gets better and better," Kate said. "I'm really looking forward to a wedding for once. I can't wait to see what the priest comes up with tomorrow."

"Well, I'm counting down the hours until it's over," I said. "Lady and Kitty can't think up any more ridiculous errands for us after tomorrow."

"Finally," Kate said. "The light at the end of the funnel."

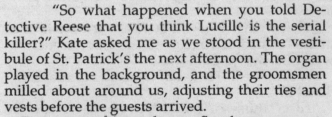

Chapter 32

"So what happened when you told Detective Reese that you think Lucille is the serial killer?" Kate asked me as we stood in the vestibule of St. Patrick's the next afternoon. The organ played in the background, and the groomsmen milled about around us, adjusting their ties and vests before the guests arrived.

Enormous white and green floral arrangements flanked the doors to the sanctuary and filled the entrance with the pungent perfume of lilies. Matching clusters of white blooms tied with mint green satin ribbon had been tied to the end of every other pew, creating a floral pathway to the altar. The altar, which had been so stark and serene the night before, could hardly be seen amidst the profusion of flowers at the front of the church.

We'd been so busy with the wedding preparations in the morning that I'd barely had time to give Kate the details of my conversation with Reese the night before. Now that we were at the church, we had time to breathe before the ceremony started.

"He was skeptical to say the least."

Kate pulled a handful of cream-colored programs tied with brown satin ribbon out of a box. "You're kidding? He thinks you're making it up?"

"Not necessarily," I said. "But he doesn't think I have any evidence."

"What about her confession? Doesn't that count for something?"

"It wasn't really a confession of murder. More like Lucille complaining about some of the victims."

"Which gives her motive," Kate said. "Plus she was at every crime scene so she had opportunity."

"That's what I said, but Reese reminded me that other people were at all the crime scenes as well. Like Byron, Gail, and us."

Kate recoiled. "He doesn't consider us suspects, does he?"

"I don't think so," I said. "But you never can tell with Reese. He's such a stickler for doing things by the book."

Kate watched me rearrange the programs she'd fanned out on a table into two even piles. "Where have I seen that before?"

I stopped readjusting the programs and put my hands on my hips. "I'm not as bad as he is. I can be spontaneous."

Kate looked at her watch. "Where are we on the schedule?"

I pulled the wedding day timeline from my suit pocket and scanned down the page. "Let's see. It's two-thirty. The bridal party is here and

tucked away, the organist is upstairs playing, and
the guests should start arriving any minute."

Kate pointed at the paper. "You forgot to put
a check mark next to '2:25—programs set out in
foyer.'"

I took out a pen and put another check mark on
the schedule. "Good catch, Kate."

She crossed her arms in front of her. "I rest my
case."

I folded the schedule in half and slid it back in
my pocket. "Wedding days don't count. Brides
pay me to be an obsessive compulsive neurotic
for one day."

"Then you should charge more," Kate said.
"You're very good at it."

"And you could stand to be a little more neurotic and a little less va-va-voom." I gave her outfit the once-over. "Would you like me to start with
the too short skirt or the practically see-through
blouse?"

Kate opened her mouth, then closed it again
and decided to change the subject back to the
murders. "So Reese told you that you were crazy
and that was it."

"No," I said. "He promised me he would question Lucille today as long as I promised not to
question anyone else."

"Who could you question while you're running
a wedding?" Kate asked. "No one involved in the
case is working with us today aside from Richard
and Fern."

"That's what I said. Unless we need to go buy a
spare guest book, we shouldn't have any contact
with potential killers."

"If we need another guest book we'll make it," Kate said. "I think we should avoid run-ins with crazy people as much as possible."

"I can't believe this is happening," Fern cried as he rushed toward us looking very Edwardian in a snug fitting black velvet suit with a stand-up collar.

"So much for avoiding crazies," Kate said.

I took Fern by the shoulders. "Calm down. What's the matter?"

"I ran out of hair spray." Fern held up a metal cylinder and shook it. Nothing. "I packed double since the bride is from Texas but I still ran out. I planned for the ten Texas bridesmaids but I didn't figure on six girls in the house party as well. This is a nightmare."

"House party?" Kate said.

Fern waved a hand in the air. "The second stringers. Like runner-up bridesmaids. If one bridesmaid can't fulfill her duties, these girls can step in."

"Close enough," I said. "It's a Texas tradition, remember? Lady explained it to us. They don't wear bridesmaids' dresses but they get a small bouquet and sit together on the second pew."

Kate snapped her fingers. "They help greet guests and hand out programs but don't have to wear matching jewelry, right? Now I remember. It sounded like a better gig than being a brides-maid."

"Well, they're not coming to greet guests until I can get their hair pageant perfect. Half of the girls in there were Miss Texas something or other."

I reached behind the propped open sanctuary

door and produced my metal emergency kit. I knelt down and snapped it open, folding out the stair-step tiers of compartments. Each level of the case held small boxes or bags of emergency supplies. Everything from straight pins, safety pins, and bobby pins, to fake rings, a dozen different colors of thread, and aspirin.

"Voilà." I held up a miniature plastic bottle of hair spray.

Fern took it and examined it. "Well, this should do half of a head."

"Make it last," I said. "We have to start the ceremony on time, so those girls are coming down the aisle at three o'clock whether they're ready or not."

"I'll do what I can." Fern fanned himself. "Do I look red? Stress gives me hives."

"You're fine." I gave him a push. "You have less than half an hour."

Fern shrieked and hurried off, then spun around on his heels. "I almost forgot. The mother of the groom asked me to tell you that the priest didn't get in the limo with the groomsmen. She hasn't seen him at all today."

Kate turned to me, her mouth gaping open. "Have you seen the priest?"

I shook my head. "He was supposed to ride over with the guys." I looked at my watch and felt my pulse start to race. The ceremony started in less than half an hour and we had no priest. Who said that being stalked by a killer was more stressful than a wedding?

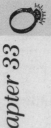

"This had better be good, Annabelle. I'm in the middle of setup and once again I have the Tweedledums of the waiter world. Every time I painstakingly arrange a table so that the light hits it just right, someone comes along and moves it," Richard said. Then his voice receded and I knew he held the phone away while bellowing to his staff. "If anyone moves these tables again, I will personally see to it that you never work in this town for the rest of your natural lives."

Richard was catering the part of the Winchester reception being held at the Decatur House, so guests wouldn't get to him for several hours. I looked at my watch. His nervous breakdown was right on schedule.

I pressed my cell phone to my ear so I could hear him better. "I need you to do me a huge favor. It's a matter of life or death."

"Really?" I knew that would get his attention. Richard was drawn to drama like a moth to a flame.

"Well, no," I admitted. "But it is a really huge wedding emergency."

"Oh please," Richard sighed. "We're not saving lives here. It's only a wedding."

"I dare you to say that to a bride."

Richard mumbled something incoherent but undoubtedly snippy.

"I need you to run across the street to the Hay-Adams and find the priest. If you don't, this wedding is going to run late, and that means everything will run late. Including your dinner service." I knew I had him there. He hated the thought of getting off schedule even more than I did.

"You lost the priest?" Richard gasped.

"We didn't lose him. We never had him. He didn't get in the limo like he was supposed to. I'm afraid he overslept or got confused and is waiting in the hotel."

"Okay, okay." I could hear him snapping his fingers. "People, people. I'm going across the street and will be right back. Don't even think of slacking off. I expect this place to be shipshape when I return."

"Thanks, Richard. You saved my life."

"I just know those waiters are going to wait for me to get back before they lift a finger. I wouldn't be surprised if they whip out pallets and take naps."

I heard the sounds of street traffic as he left the Decatur House for the hotel. "Don't you think you're a little tough on them?"

"The last time I let a waiter take a break during a wedding because he wasn't feeling well, I found him ten minutes later making out with the bride in a coat closet. Mark my words, Annabelle. If you let them, they'll walk all over you."

"You're kidding? What happened to the bride and the waiter?"

"Who knows what happened to the bride? She's probably in a meaningful relationship with her yard boy. Not that I blamed her. The groom was a toad. But I'll tell you one thing—that waiter never worked for me again."

I shook my head. "Juicy things like that never happen at my weddings."

"That was nothing compared to the time I found the sexy divorcée mother of the bride in her car with a groomsman. Neither of them had on a stitch of clothing. Now that's something I wish I'd never seen. You won't catch me going in parking garages alone anymore."

"What did you do?"

"What could I do?" Richard said. "I tapped on the window and handed her the final bill."

I stifled a laugh. "I'll bet she paid up."

"And gave me a nice tip on top of it. Okay, I'm at the Hay-Adams. How do I find this priest?"

"Do you see anyone who looks like a priest waiting in the lobby?"

"If someone was sitting here in a priest collar, I think I could have figured it out, Annabelle." Richard gave me an impatient sigh. "There's no one here. What name is the room under?"

"O'Malley. Father O'Malley. Explain things to the concierge and see if he'll give you the room number."

"This should be easy. I know this concierge. I think I've seen him at the Crow Bar before. It's hard to tell since he's not in leather, though."

"Could we focus on finding the priest?"

"Fine," Richard snapped, and then I heard muffled voices and laughter. This could take a while if Richard got caught up in a conversation and forgot why he was there. After a few minutes he came back on the line. "Got it. I'm on my way upstairs right now."

I heard the elevator chimes. "Good work. Usually they won't give the room numbers out to just anyone."

"Might I remind you that I am not just anyone, darling. Not only did I get the room number, but I also got a date for next week."

"How come you can date someone who wears leather but I can't?" I protested.

"Do you have to ask?" Richard said. "This Ian fellow is no good for you, Annabelle. Mark my words."

Great. Dating advice from someone who frequented the Crow Bar.

"Okay, I'm here. Room 326. The door is standing open a bit."

"Maybe he left the door open because he expected someone to come get him for the wedding," I said. "Go on in."

"Yoo hoo," Richard called. "Father O'Malley. I'm here to take you to—" Richard sucked in his breath.

"What's the matter?" I asked. "He's not there?"

"I don't see him." Richard's voice shook as he spoke. "But I do see something splattered on the carpet."

I felt very light-headed, and I clutched the phone tighter. "What do you mean?"

"Annabelle, I think it's blood."

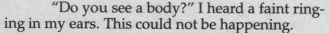

Chapter 34

"Do you see a body?" I heard a faint ringing in my ears. This could not be happening.

"No," Richard said. "And you're out of your mind if you think I'm going to run around looking for one. Unlike some people I know, I'm not interested in becoming the next Nancy Drew."

I lowered myself onto a bench in an alcove off the church vestibule. "How much blood is there?"

"Well, he didn't just get a paper cut," Richard said. "Now if you don't mind, I'm getting out of here and calling the police."

Richard screamed, and I heard the phone clatter to the floor.

"Richard? Are you okay? What's happening?" There were muffled voices in the background. One voice brimmed with impatience. Obviously Richard's. Had a maid walked in and startled him?

"I'm fine," Richard said after he finally retrieved the phone. "I found the priest."

I sucked in my breath. "You found the body? Where was it?"

"Not the body. The priest. He's alive and well."

I almost slipped off the bench. "What do you mean he's alive? What about all the blood?"

"It appears that he had a few accidents shaving and it smells like he got very drunk before he did it." Richard kept his voice low. "He's in the bathroom trying to clean up, but I don't know how much good it will do."

"How bad does he look?"

"His face is covered with bits of toilet tissue from where he attempted to stop the bleeding. If you ask me, it looks like he tried to papier-mâché himself."

I rubbed my temple with one hand. "He must have gotten into the bottle of Irish whiskey that we left in his room."

"He didn't only get into it, Annabelle, he finished it," Richard said. "The empty bottle is sitting right here on the desk."

"That's impossible," I said. "It was a huge bottle."

"No kidding. Is it a new Wedding Belles tradition to encourage guests to get drunk *before* the wedding?"

"No," I said. "The groom's mother requested we put it in his room as a welcome touch."

"Nothing says welcome more graciously than a huge bottle of booze," Richard said. "What happened to a nice fruit basket?"

"They're Irish," I explained. "I don't think fruit says welcome to them like whiskey does."

"I'd better go," Richard whispered. "He came out of the bathroom and he doesn't look too steady on his feet."

I rubbed my head. "Will he be able to perform the ceremony?"

"Do you have a backup priest on call?"

"Of course not," I said. "When have you ever heard of needing a backup priest?"

"Then I guess he'll have to do, won't he?" Richard asked.

"Can you drive him over to St. Patrick's?" I looked at my watch. "We don't have time to send a limo back for him."

"I just got my car detailed," Richard protested.

"What could he possibly do to your car, Richard?"

"Bleed on it, for one."

I rolled my eyes. "They're shaving cuts, for heaven's sake. It's not like he was in a knife fight."

"Fine," Richard said. "But I'm taking one of the hotel's towels for him to sit on. They can bill me."

"Hurry," I said, and hung up.

I slipped the cell phone into my suit pocket and tried to plaster a smile on my face as I walked back into the church vestibule.

The church entrance buzzed with activity as guests poured in for the ceremony. Kate greeted people with a program as they entered the church and directed them to the line of a dozen or so waiting groomsmen. The tuxedoed groomsman at the head of the line offered his arm as a female guest approached and then escorted her down the aisle, while the next groomsman stepped up and took his place. I smiled. These guys had actually paid attention during Kate's ushering "boot camp" last night. At least one part of the wedding was going well.

I walked up behind Kate. "No sign of the house party yet?"

"Let's hope Fern gets them ready in time for the reception," Kate said. "Any luck with the priest?"

"Kind of. Richard's bringing him, but he's drunk."

Kate's mouth fell open. "Richard is drunk?"

"No, the priest is drunk," I said.

Kate's face registered comprehension. "I guess that's worse, huh?"

"For our immediate purposes? Yes."

"Don't worry," Kate said. "He was drunk last night and he managed to run the rehearsal."

"I thought you said he told dirty jokes and the bride's side was livid?"

Kate bit her bottom lip. "I didn't say he ran it well, but he got the job done."

"So if I lower my expectations, I'll be happier?"

Kate shrugged. "It works for me."

"So far this is not going as seamlessly as I'd hoped."

Kate cringed. "I hate to tell you this, then, but Detective Reese called while you were talking to Richard."

I felt a twinge of jealousy. "Reese called you?"

"He tried your cell but I guess he got voice mail," Kate said. "Anyway, he went to the Wedding Shoppe to talk to Lucille."

"What did she say when he asked her about the murders?"

"That's the problem. He couldn't ask her about the murders because she wasn't there. The sales clerk said she didn't show up for work in the morning and didn't answer when they called her house looking for her. They're looking for her but no luck so far."

My stomach clenched into a knot. The person I was sure had already killed three other wedding planners and had tried to kill me was missing. Suddenly an intoxicated priest was only one of my problems.

Chapter 35

"A little help would be nice." Richard stuck his head inside the church foyer.

I let out a deep breath as Kate and I rushed to the door. "You got here just in time. We seated the last of the guests and sent the groomsmen back to the sacristy two minutes ago."

"Good," Richard said. "The fewer people who see this, the better." He stepped inside holding Father O'Malley up by the arm.

I gasped. The ruddy-cheeked priest had blood trickling down his face and neck onto his black robes. The gobs of toilet paper stuck to his face in patches had done little to stop the bleeding. It looked like he'd nicked an artery.

"What happened?" Kate's mouth gaped open.

"I forgot to tell you that he tried to shave after finishing off the bottle of whiskey in his hotel room," I said under my breath.

Kate raised an eyebrow. "Minor detail, I guess."

"Don't worry about me, lassies." Father O'Malley let go of Richard and gave us a dazzling smile. "Only a scratch or two. It looks worse than it is."

I certainly hoped so.

Father O'Malley ran a hand through his bushy white hair and cast a glazed look around the foyer. "I'd better get back to the sacristy. You can't start without me, now can you?"

He teetered off down the aisle, and I turned to Kate. "Can you follow him and make sure he actually makes it back there?"

Kate took off after him, walking more steadily in three-inch spike heels than the stumbling priest.

"Well, my job's done." Richard headed for the door. "I have to get back to the Decatur House before the waiters set the place on fire."

I clutched his arm. "Can't you stay and help with the processional?"

Richard tried to shake my hand off. "I hate processionals. That's why I'm a caterer and you're a wedding planner."

"Have a little sympathy, Richard. I have a drunken priest and a dozen bridesmaids from Texas."

Richard slapped at my hand. "Now why would that make me want to stay?"

"There are only two children, and you won't even have to touch them." I gave him my best puppy dog eyes. "It will take five minutes. I promise."

Richard threw his hands in the air. "Fine, but I'm only doing this for the potential entertainment value. I want to see the look on everyone's face when the priest walks out."

I gave him a quick hug. "I owe you big-time."

He smoothed the front of his black button-down shirt where I'd wrinkled it. "I'll add it to your tab."

"They're ready," Fern called as he led a line of very blond women toward us. The house party walked in front wearing black cocktail dresses in various styles, and the bridesmaids followed in long, chocolate brown gowns with a mint green ribbon tied around their waists. All the girls wore their hair swept up in French twists and each had on a single strand of pearls.

"Good God," Richard said. "The Stepford Wives ride again."

I elbowed him. I had to admit that they did look remarkably like a set of plastic bridesmaids you could buy to put on wedding cakes.

"Where are the mothers?" I asked Fern when he reached me.

"Still fussing over the bride," he sighed. "Do you need them?"

I looked at my watch. We were running five minutes behind. "Yes, we need to send them down the aisle right now."

Fern stifled a squeal and hurried away.

"Can you run up and cue the organist for the seating of the mothers?" I asked Richard.

"Run? In this outfit? I don't think so. Why don't you run up and I'll get everyone ready to walk?" Richard gave my black evening suit the once-over. "That is polyester, after all, isn't it?"

I glared at him. "I'll have you know that this is from Ann Taylor and it's one hundred percent silk."

Richard eyed me again. "Not bad, darling, but Prada trumps Ann Taylor any day."

"Fine." I handed him my wedding schedule and headed for the stairs. "But the mothers had better be lined up and ready to go when I get back."

Richard gave me his most sugary smile and waved me away. "Tick tock, Annabelle. Tick tock."

I took the spiral stairs to the balcony two at a time and caught my breath when I reached the top. I stuck my head in the doorway and caught the eye of the organist. "We're ready for the mothers' song." I turned around and ran back down the stairs. When I reached the bottom, Richard stood with both of the mothers' escorts at the back of the aisle, but no mothers.

"Don't look at me," he said. "Fern was in charge of getting them here."

"Here we are." Fern sounded out of breath as he walked up with the mothers of the bride and groom in tow. "We had a slight delay because of some last minute wardrobe changes." He gave me a look that said not to ask.

"Don't you think Mrs. Kelly looks fabulous in this stole?" Kitty asked, turning the mother of the groom around so I could admire the beige satin wrap. With it tied in front, you could barely see the hot pink strapless gown with rows of long fringe that Mrs. Kelly had chosen. I'm sure that was Kitty's entire objective.

"I thought it might be a little much," the groom's mother said, trying to rearrange the front of the wrap. "But Kitty insisted that the mothers should coordinate."

Kitty smiled, clearly satisfied with herself. She, too, wore a wrap. Of course, hers matched her gray satin gown perfectly and sat slightly off the shoulder.

"You both look lovely," I said, and prodded them into place next to their escorts.

The sound of "Ave Maria" filled the church, and I nudged Mrs. Kelly to start down the aisle.

Kitty pulled me close to her. "How is everything so far?"

"Perfect," I lied.

Kitty beamed at me as she looked at the flower filled sanctuary. "I want this to be a wedding that no one will ever forget."

"I'm sure people will be talking about it for years," I said, and smiled back to Kitty as I sent her down the aisle.

I watched from the corner of my eye as Father O'Malley led the groom and groomsmen from the sacristy to the altar, swaying as he walked. "We have to speed up this processional before the priest keels over," I whispered to Richard.

I motioned to Fern to bring up the house party while I ran to the stairwell again. I pulled myself up the stairs to the balcony and gave a wave to the organist when I reached the top. "Bridesmaids," I said, then spun on my heel and ran down again while the music changed.

Richard stood to the side of the double doors, nodding to each girl to indicate when she should walk, while Fern gave their hair a final spritz with hair spray. The house party had almost reached the end of the aisle, and the bridesmaids were beginning their processional. I wondered if Guinness had a category for fastest wedding processional.

I waited until Fern pushed the flower girl and ring bearer to the doors, then I dragged myself back up the stairs and paused at the top to suck in air. I managed to nod at the organist and mouth the word "bride" before heading back down again.

When I came out of the stairwell panting for breath, Lady stood off to the side of the aisle holding her father's arm, while Fern fussed with the hem of her dress. She looked like a cross between a princess and a drag queen in her heavy pageant makeup and halo of teased blond hair. Now I understood why Fern had run out of hair spray, and I was surprised he hadn't run out of eye shadow as well.

Fern looked over his shoulder at me. "She has something on the bottom of her dress."

I knelt down next to him and noticed that he had my emergency kit open next to him. "Did you try the Shout Wipes?"

He rubbed briskly at the black spot near her hem. "That's what I'm using but they're not working fast enough."

I reached in the metal case and pulled out a piece of cream-colored chalk. I rubbed it gently over the spot to cover it. "That should work for now."

Fern looked at me in awe. "You're the wedding planner version of MacGyver."

Kate appeared in time to help Richard close the heavy double doors while Fern and I straightened the bride's cathedral-length veil. Lady rested her hand lightly on her father's arm and held her white teardrop-shaped bouquet in the other. Unlike most brides, her hands weren't shaking. Years of pageant training came in handy.

The fanfare to "Trumpet Voluntary" began, and Richard and Kate flung open the doors. Lady produced a runway perfect smile and threw her shoulders back as she began her walk down the long aisle. Kate and Richard closed the doors after her and we all let out a breath.

I slumped against the door. "The hard part is over."

"For you, maybe," Richard said. "I still have the whole reception to go."

"I need to get more hair spray before the reception," Fern said. "Is there a drugstore nearby?"

"You're kidding, right?" I asked, watching through the glass cutouts in the doors as the bride reached the altar. "Not even gale force winds could move that hair."

"As riveting as this is, I've got to run." Richard took a few steps backward. "I'll see you back at the Decatur House."

"Should we warn him?" Kate asked. "In case she shows up?"

Richard stopped. "In case who shows up? Are you sending one of your brides to see the reception decor?"

"Not exactly," I said. "The police are looking for Lucille as a suspect in the murders but haven't been able to find her yet."

"That sweet little old lady? Why would she show up at the Decatur House?"

"Well, she did try to kill Annabelle once already," Kate said. "She might try to finish the job."

"How would she know where to find you?" Richard asked.

I dropped my eyes to the floor. "I told her where my wedding was being held, but that was before I knew that she was the killer."

"Great," Richard grumbled. "Not only do I have to deal with simpleton waiters, I might have a lunatic murderer crash my party."

"Don't be so dramatic," I said. "It could be worse."

Richard's eyes widened as he looked past me. "Too late."

I turned around and peered through the glass in the sanctuary doors. A crowd had gathered at the altar.

"I guess the priest lost more blood than I thought," Richard said. "He just fainted."

I'd been right when I'd told Kitty that this would be a wedding no one would ever forget.

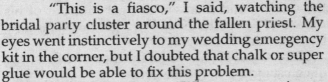

Chapter 36

"This is a fiasco," I said, watching the bridal party cluster around the fallen priest. My eyes went instinctively to my wedding emergency kit in the corner, but I doubted that chalk or super glue would be able to fix this problem.

Kate clutched my arm. "What are we going to do?"

"I don't know," I said. "He clearly can't finish the ceremony, and I doubt that there's an ordained minister in the crowd."

"I'm ordained," Fern said.

We all stared at him, mouths open.

"You?" Richard managed to say. "Since when?"

Fern crossed his arms in front of his chest. "Since they started ordaining people over the Internet. I thought it might come in handy one day."

I grabbed Fern by the shoulders. "So you can legally marry people?"

"Of course." He tapped his fingers on his chin.

"I haven't actually performed a ceremony yet, though."

"There's a first time for everything," I said. "Do you think you can finish the wedding?"

Fern raised an eyebrow. "Would I get to wear robes?"

"Sure," I said, avoiding Richard's disapproving look. "We can get you robes."

Fern's eyes danced. "I've always wanted to wear ceremonial robes."

"This is your plan?" Richard said. "You're going to have the hairdresser officiate the ceremony?"

"Unless you have a better idea," I said. "Kate can get the groomsmen to drag the priest back to the sacristy and then we can get him out of his robes and Fern into them. We'll get this ceremony back on track in no time."

Richard put his hands on his hips. "With a drag queen standing in for the priest?"

"I beg your pardon," Fern said.

"Do you or do you not have a green Jackie Kennedy suit and matching pillbox hat?" Richard asked.

"Green?" Fern gasped. "I'll have you know that it's peacock blue and it looks stunning on me."

Kate looked intrigued. "You do?"

"I think I've proved my point," Richard said.

My cell phone buzzed in my pocket and I turned to Kate. "I'd better answer this in case it's another wedding emergency. Can you handle the priest and Fern?"

"Don't worry, Annie. I'm on it." She grabbed Fern by the arm and started off down the aisle.

I flipped open the phone. "Wedding Belles. This is Annabelle."

"I'm glad I found you."

The voice sounded familiar, but I couldn't place it right away. "Who is this?" I asked.

"It's Mike, I mean Detective Reese."

"Hi, Detective." I tried not to sound too pleasantly surprised. "I'm kind of in the middle of a wedding."

"I know. I wouldn't bother you if it wasn't important."

I looked nervously through the sanctuary doors. Kate's flirting seemed to be working because the groomsmen lifted the priest and carried him to the sacristy door behind the altar.

"I'm glad you called." I said. "I forgot to mention something to you on my earlier message. If Lucille has any desire to finish the job she started with Margery, you should check on her at the hospital. She could be in danger."

"Margery isn't in danger from Lucille."

Typical. "Because you didn't think of it?"

"No." Reese sounded impatient. "I don't think Margery is in danger because we found Lucille."

"Good Lord." Richard pointed to the altar as Fern walked out in black robes with an enormous silver cross around his neck that looked like it had been pulled off a wall. Obviously his own touch.

"Dearly beloved." Fern opened his arms in a sweeping motion. We are gathered here today in the sight of God and these fabulously dressed witnesses."

"I hate being right all the time," Richard muttered.

"What?" I couldn't focus on Reese completely with Fern on stage. "Oh, you found Lucille? Well, that's a relief."

"Not exactly," Reese said. "She's dead."

My mouth went dry and I tore my eyes away from Fern. "What do you mean?"

"We found her at her house strangled to death. Exactly like the other victims."

"It doesn't make sense." I shook my head. "If Lucille was strangled to death, then who's the killer?"

"I guess that's the million dollar question."

Chapter 37

"Are you there, Annabelle?" Reese asked.

I nodded mutely, and then gave myself a mental shake. "I'm here. I think I'm in shock."

"You should be in shock. Are you watching this?" Richard asked, gaping at the drama unfolding at the front of the church.

Fern had picked up the ceremony in the middle of the vows, where Father O'Malley had left off. "For better or for worse, for richer not poorer ..."

He paused for the bride to repeat after him. Not completely inappropriate vows, nonetheless I was glad I couldn't see Kitty's face.

"I'm sending an officer over to the church," Reese said.

"Do you really think that's necessary?" I didn't relish the idea of a police car outside the church, but the way this wedding was going, who knew if anyone would even notice?

"In sickness and in wealth ..."

"Like you said, the killer may want to finish the

job," Reese said. "I'm sending one to Margery's hospital room, too."

"Okay," I said numbly. "If you think it's a good idea. I'd better go before the ceremony ends."

"Be careful, Annabelle," Reese said. "There's still a killer on the loose."

I dropped the phone in my pocket after hanging up. "Lucille is dead."

"What?" Richard said. "I thought she was the bad guy."

"Apparently not." I felt very light-headed. "She's been murdered just like the others."

Richard wagged a finger at me. "I told you she was too sweet-looking. You never believe me."

I blinked back a tear as I thought of the kind, grandmotherly wedding planner. I felt awful for even thinking that she could have killed someone.

"She was too fragile to strangle someone anyway," Richard said. "She must have been about sixty, right?"

"Yes, but Leatrice is eighty and I wouldn't consider her fragile."

Richard rolled his eyes. "Leatrice is not a normal little old lady in any sense of the word."

"True," I admitted. "But if Lucille didn't do it, who did?"

"Your suspects are a dying breed," Richard said. "If you wait long enough, you'll know who the murderer is because it will be the only person left alive."

"If I wait any longer, I won't be left alive." I brushed a loose strand of hair off my face. "If only we could find a pattern to the murders."

"They're all wedding planners," Richard said. "I'd call that a pattern."

"But the victims don't make sense. Stephanie doesn't have any connection to everyone else. Even Lucille was an old-timer like Carolyn and Eleanor."

"You aren't part of that crowd and the killer tried to get rid of you."

"Probably because I meddled in the case," I said. "Margery is part of that group, though."

"So everyone fits except you and Stephanie," Richard said. "The killer went after you because you were trying to solve the case, so now you're just missing the reason he killed Stephanie."

"That's the answer to this whole case. I can feel it."

"Why not try to figure it out without Stephanie? If she doesn't fit, eliminate her from the equation."

I gave a weak laugh. "Maybe the killer goofed up and killed her by accident."

My breath caught in my throat. What if the killer had made a mistake and meant to kill someone else at the party? I grabbed Richard's arm. "Where was Stephanie murdered?"

Richard took a step away from me. "In Maxwell's equipment closet. Why?"

"I'm sure it's dark in there, right?"

"Closets are usually dark, Annabelle." Richard looked at me like I'd lost my mind. "That's why Maxwell was famous for his closet meetings."

"His closet meetings?" I asked. "What are you talking about?"

"Let's just say he's been caught at more than

one party with a pretty young thing in a closet."

I swatted at him. "Why didn't you tell me this earlier?"

"Ouch." Richard rubbed his arm where I hit him. "I assumed it was common knowledge. Maxwell isn't the most discreet person in the world."

"What if Maxwell set up two closet meetings at the party and the killer only knew about one?"

Richard rapped his fingers on his chin. "I wouldn't put a ménage à trois past Maxwell."

"Stephanie doesn't look very much like the other planners, though. Even in the dark."

"With her wild curly hair, it would be hard to mistake for any of the older planners, that's for sure," Richard agreed. "They're the queens of the frumpy bob."

I frowned and looked through the sanctuary doors at the long line of groomsmen and bridesmaids. From where I stood they looked like two rows of human clones since all the men wore identical tuxedoes and all the women had matching gowns and blond French twists.

I snapped my fingers. "Wait a second. Stephanie didn't have her hair down at the party. She wore it up."

"You're right," Richard said. "I remember thinking she looked more subdued than usual."

"With her hair up, she could easily pass for another wedding planner," I said. "Especially in the dark."

"Doesn't Gail wear her hair up all the time?" Richard asked. "She certainly falls in the same category as the other victims."

"And she used to have a thing with Maxwell, and she argued with him at the party," I said.

"Even if the killer intended to kill Gail instead of Stephanie, that doesn't tell us who the killer is," Richard said. "We're right back where we started."

I glanced through the doors again. "And the ceremony is going to end any minute."

"If Fern ever wraps up his homily," Richard said. "Who knew you could stretch a metaphor about marriage and fashion for so long?"

"I need to run to the bridal room and get the bride's things before she and the groom come out and get in their car," I said. "This is one bride who will notice if her makeup bag isn't there. Can you stay here and open the doors if they come out?"

Richard gave a mock bow. "I live to serve."

I made a face at him as I headed down the side of the church to the bride's holding room. Not surprisingly, the room looked like a war zone. Garment bags were draped over chairs and makeup littered the large wooden table in the center of the room. Finding the bride's tiny white cosmetic bag wasn't going to be as easy as I thought.

I pawed through the duffel bags scattered on the sagging green upholstered couch in the corner and found the black bag I'd seen the bride arrive with. Her makeup bag had to be inside. I tugged on the zipper but it wouldn't open. I jiggled it and tried again. Crap. It was stuck. I looked at the clock on the wall and pulled harder. Nothing. By the time I got it open, the bride would be long gone. I tried not to panic. Who was good at opening things? Not Richard. He might wrinkle his outfit. Not Kate. She might break a nail. I wished I was stronger.

Then it dawned on me who was known for her strength. My heart started pounding. Why hadn't I thought of it earlier? I knew who could strangle someone and push them over a balcony and who had been at every crime scene. Plus, she had a connection to all the victims except for Stephanie. Now I was sure that Stephanie had been a mistake, because the killer didn't have the best eyesight. It would have been easy for her to mistake Stephanie for someone else in a dark closet. I dropped the duffel bag and reached for my cell phone.

"Hello, Annabelle."

I looked up and sucked in my breath. Margery.

Chapter 38

"Surprised to see me?" Margery took a step inside the room.

I swallowed hard. "Shouldn't you be at the hospital?"

Margery laughed harshly. "Recovering from my fake concussion?"

"I'm not sure what you mean." I tried to speed dial Richard on my cell phone without looking. "I'm glad to see you up and about, though."

"I doubt that." Margery took a step toward me. She wore the same brown suit that she'd worn at the Mayflower, but today she looked disheveled and a bit crazy. "Surely by now you've figured it out, haven't you, Sherlock?"

"Figured what out?" I took a few steps to the side so the table stood between us.

"From what Lucille said, I was sure you were on to me. When she called me after you left the Wedding Shoppe, I knew that you were too close for comfort."

I tried to remember if Lucille had said anything incriminating about Margery. "Lucille didn't say anything about you. Honest."

"I find that hard to believe." Margery pulled one of the plastic garment bags off a chair and pulled it taut. "When she told me that you came by the store for a flower girl's basket, I knew that you must be pumping her for information. You probably didn't even have a flower girl in the wedding."

"But I did need a flower girl basket," I said. "Did you kill Lucille because you thought she told me something about you?"

Margery twisted the plastic into a coil. "Lucille knew too much, even if she didn't know that she did. She heard me talking to my lawyer on the phone about the shop and eventually she would have put it all together."

"So what if Lucille knew you talked to a lawyer about taking Carolyn's husband to court?"

Margery laughed. "Maybe I gave you too much credit. I wasn't taking Mr. Crabbe to court. I was buying the business from him."

I staggered back a few steps. "You're the secret buyer?"

"It wouldn't have been secret forever. There's no crime in buying a business from a willing seller, and with Carolyn gone, her husband was more than willing to get the store off his hands."

I couldn't hide my shock. "You have enough money to buy the entire business?"

Margery's face twitched. "I've socked away my money for years, and Lucille gave me some of her savings to invest. Between the two of us, we have a nice nest egg. More than anyone would have expected."

I felt sick thinking of poor Lucille and felt sicker looking at the plastic that Margery held between her hands. Did she plan on strangling me with it? I edged around the table away from her.

"Lucille's nest egg didn't end up doing her much good," I said. "Did she know about what you were doing with her money?"

"I planned to tell her. I wanted us to run the business together. But things didn't work out."

"Why did you have to kill her? She didn't know anything," I insisted. "She talked about how much she missed you and how worried she was."

A look of genuine regret flickered across Margery's face. "I did it for both of us, you know. But Lucille never would have understood."

I darted a look at my phone but couldn't tell if it had connected or not. "Did what for both of you?"

Margery gave an exasperated sigh. "Surely you've put two and two together by now?"

"You killed everyone for Lucille and then you killed her, too?" I took a step around the corner of the table and Margery followed.

"Don't say it like that!" Margery yelled, slamming a hand down on the table. "Lucille wasn't supposed to die."

"So why did you kill her, then?" If I could keep Margery talking, maybe Reese's police guard would arrive before she tried to add me to her list of victims.

"She was going to ruin everything I'd done for us. She knew I'd been missing at all the crime scenes right before the bodies were found even though she would never admit it to herself. I always gave her a good excuse, but if anyone dug deeper, Lucille could incriminate me without even trying."

"I get that you killed Carolyn so you could buy the business, but why kill other wedding planners? What did they ever do to you? And what about Stephanie?"

Margery's face reddened. "Stephanie was a mistake. She shouldn't have been wearing her hair like Gail does. They looked exactly alike."

"Especially without your glasses, right?" I said. "Lucille mentioned that you don't like to wear your glasses but you're blind without them."

"Very clever." Margery wagged a finger at me. "I regret Stephanie but I'm not sorry for the others. Lucille and I slaved away under Carolyn for years with the promise that she'd make us partners one day. That day never came. While every other planner left the Wedding Shoppe and became successful, we stayed with Carolyn."

I nodded, finally understanding. "You thought your years of loyalty would pay off but instead you were looked down upon by all the planners who passed through the store."

Margery balled her hands into fists. "I trained them all and they became fancy planners while Lucille and I did Carolyn's dirty work for twenty years."

"So you killed them because they left and you didn't?" I punched Richard's number again. "That doesn't seem very fair."

"Fair?" Margery advanced on me, snapping

her makeshift plastic rope. "Don't you think I heard the comments they made about us? They all acted like they were better than us and didn't give us the time of day. No one cared about what we thought. We were only Carolyn's lowly assistants, and Carolyn made sure to keep us in our place."

"The old-timers are mean to everyone." I took a baby step toward the door. "Do you think they've been welcoming to us, either?"

Margery's shoulders sagged. "That's why I thought you might understand. You and Kate were treated badly as well."

"I do understand," I said. "There have been plenty of times that I've felt the same way you do."

Margery's face softened, then she set her mouth and gave her head a shake. "No, you're trying to trick me. If you didn't like Carolyn or Eleanor why were you so set on finding out who killed them?"

I moved around the table, closer to the door. A few more feet and I could make a run for it. "I thought that if someone was killing wedding planners, I might be next."

"You would have been next if the bust hadn't slipped in my hands at the last minute. You weren't supposed to survive, but the marble proved to be tricky to hold." She snapped the plastic. "I much prefer strangulation."

How comforting. "You hit yourself to throw people off your trail?"

Margery looked pleased with herself. "I made sure to give myself a nasty looking gash, but nothing more serious than that. Not bad for a wedding planner's assistant, don't you think? No one would suspect one of the killer's victims."

I had to admit that it was pretty clever.

Margery made a clucking sound and took another step toward me. "You should have left well enough alone, Annabelle. Now you are going to be the next wedding planner murdered."

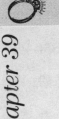

Chapter 39

"You rang?" Richard strode through the door holding his phone out in front of him and looking agitated. "One call would have been enough, you know. You didn't have to harass me."

Margery spun around, and I took advantage of the distraction to bolt for the door. It took Margery a second to react and chase after me. "Run, Richard, run!"

Richard shrieked when he saw me heading straight for him, followed by Margery holding a plastic rope between her outstretched arms. He turned around and took off down the hallway, his arms above his head.

"What the hell is going on?" he yelled over his shoulder. "Why are you chasing me?"

"I'm not chasing you. Margery is chasing us!"

Richard rounded the corner. "Why?"

"She's the killer!" I looked over my shoulder and gave Richard a push. "And she's gaining on us!"

We tore into the church foyer, and I could hear Fern wrapping up the ceremony.

"By the power invested in me by Ordination. com ..."

"Outside," I screamed to Richard, shoving him toward the doors. "Hurry!"

We burst through the doors, and I saw the police car pulling up in front of the church.

"Help!" Richard cried. "She's after me!"

He ran to the police officer, who leapt out of the car with his gun drawn.

"Not me." I pointed behind me. "It's her."

Margery skidded to a stop when she saw the officer, then turned and ran toward the street.

"Don't let her get away," I cried to the officer, and then took off after her.

Richard followed me. "Now we're chasing her?"

Margery darted across the street without looking. In a flash I saw her bounce off the hood of a silver SUV and land on the pavement. The driver of the SUV jumped out of the car while traffic screeched to a stop around Margery.

I rushed over and knelt beside Margery with Richard behind me while the police officer radioed for an ambulance from his squad car. As I looked at Margery's twisted neck and blood trickling out the corner of her mouth, I knew it was too late.

I looked up at Richard. "She's dead." I sat back on my heels and covered my face with my hands.

"What? You're sad?" Richard bent over at the waist, panting for breath. "Might I remind you that she just tried to kill both of us."

The church doors opened and the sound of festive organ music spilled out along with the bride and groom, followed by the bridal party and families. Everyone stopped and stared at the flashing lights of the police car and the body in the street. Kitty's mouth hung open as Kate and Fern pushed through the crowd and hurried forward.

The police officer looked up at Fern as he approached us. "At least the priest can administer last rites."

Richard's eyebrows popped up and disappeared beneath his bangs. "It's official. I'm in hell."

Fern pressed his hands together in a prayer pose. "Did I hear someone call for a priest?"

Richard pointed a warning finger at him. "Don't even think about it."

Fern shook his head at Richard and whispered to the cop, "It's such a shame. No one respects the clergy these days."

Chapter 40

"I can't believe that Margery killed all those people," Kate yelled from my kitchen as she searched through the contents of my refrigerator. "There's nothing in here."

"I'm stunned," Richard said, looking up from where he lay draped across the couch.

"About Margery being a serial killer?" I asked. I was still processing the whole day and felt a bit shell-shocked. I leaned back in the armchair across from Richard and slipped off my shoes. "I can't believe she almost got away with it."

"No. I'm stunned that your refrigerator is devoid of food." He clearly was not.

"Can we order something?" Kate asked. "I'm starved. The meanie caterer didn't feed us at the wedding."

I looked at the wrought-iron clock on the wall. "If any place is still open at this hour."

"Well, I thought dinner was scrumptious," Fern

called from the bathroom, where he was touching up his hair.

"That's because you were seated at one of the guest tables and actually ate," I said. "The rest of us had to scrounge for leftover hors d'oeuvres in the kitchen."

"Might I remind you that the police kept everyone at the church for so long that once the guests got to the reception I barely had time to rush them through three courses, much less serve dinner to the staff?" Richard said. "If the band asked me for food one more time, I was going to cut their wires. Don't people eat before they come to work?"

Kate walked out from the kitchen and made a face at Richard behind him. "Those of us not lucky enough to score a seat at the head table haven't eaten all day."

"Well, they usually seat the priest at the wedding reception," Fern said, joining us in the living room. "I was only following tradition."

Richard sat up. "You weren't really the priest. How many times do I have to tell you?"

Fern ignored him. "I thought it was a lovely wedding reception. You should have tasted the rack of lamb, girls. It was divine."

"That's it," Kate said. "I'm ordering pizza."

I heard tapping at the door and started to get up when Fern waved for me to sit down again.

"I'll answer it, doll. You were running around all night. Once I gave the prayer at dinner and touched up the bride's hair, my evening was a breeze."

Fern opened the door and Leatrice bounded in.

She wore a three dimensional reindeer sweatshirt with a red light-up nose and a puffy blue menorah hat.

She plopped down on the couch next to Richard. "Tell me everything. You know they never give details on the police scanner."

"To make a long story short," I said, "the wedding planner killer is dead."

Leatrice looked enraptured as she sank back on the couch, her hat jiggling above her.

Richard eyed the hat and whispered to me, "Is that what I think it is?"

"Interesting hat, Leatrice," I said. "Where did you get it?"

"Holiday sale last year at Filene's." She reached up and patted the stuffed fabric candles. "You don't see many Christmas hats with candles, do you?"

"That's because it's a menorah," Richard muttered.

Leatrice rubbed her hands together. "So who was the killer? The sleazy photographer?"

"I wish," Kate said. "We could do with one fewer of those in this business."

"It was Margery, one of Carolyn's assistants." I said.

Leatrice scratched her head. "Margery? Was she a suspect?"

"Actually, she was one of the victims," I explained. "Or we thought she was. She was the other person hit on the head who survived."

Leatrice's eyes lit up almost as brightly as the nose on her sweater. "That was a ruse to throw people off her trail?"

"Not bad, huh?" Kate said.

Leatrice bounced up and down on the couch. "What was her motive?"

"Since Carolyn didn't make her a partner in the business like she promised, Margery plotted to kill her and buy the business from her husband. She killed the other planners because they looked down on her for being an assistant."

"You know the old saying," Kate said. "Hell has no fury like a woman's thorn."

"Margery had gone a bit insane," I said.

Richard scooted away from Leatrice. "After all those years of planning weddings, who could blame her?"

"Oh, good. Another perk of the job to look forward to," Kate said.

Leatrice clapped her hands. "I can't wait to tell Ian."

"Well, he'll be over here tomorrow," I said. "You're welcome to stop by to say hello."

"Oh, no." Leatrice shook her head. "He's on his way over tonight."

I jerked up in my seat. "How do you know?"

"Because I called him when I saw you come home. I knew he'd want to be here when we talked about the murders." She lowered her voice. "Do you know, I think we might have another case to solve? There may have been something funny in those drinks last night."

Richard raised an eyebrow. "You mean like alcohol?"

"Maybe we were drugged," Leatrice continued. "I'll bet that priest was really a spy sent to infiltrate the U.S."

Leatrice saw a conspiracy around every corner.

"A spy, indeed." Fern looked highly affronted.

"She's not talking about you," Richard said. "She's talking about the other priest."

Leatrice stared at Fern. "You're a priest?"

The doorbell rang, and I leapt up to answer it. Detective Reese stood in the hallway, his hands jammed in the pockets of his jeans. His dark blazer looked like it had been slept in.

"Oh, hi." I was surprised to see him. I looked around for Hobbes. "Do you have more questions for me, Detective?"

Reese glanced into my apartment and lowered his voice. "Actually, I just got off work after finishing all the paperwork on the wedding planner case and you were on my mind."

"Probably because I was involved in the case," I said. "I have a habit of ending up in your work a lot."

"That's not always a bad thing." He smiled at me, and his hazel eyes deepened to green. "There are certainly worse things to have on my mind."

My pulse quickened, and then I remembered that Ian was on his way over. I wasn't used to juggling two men at one time. I gulped as I returned his smile. As Kate would say, I was between a clock and a hard place.